by Henry Winkler and Lin Oliver

HANK ZIPZER

the world's greatest underachiever

Summer School!
What Genius Thought
That Up?

Grosset & Dunlap

To Jed, Zoe, and Max—who all fought
through their learning challenges and
blossomed into extraordinary people.
And always, to Stacey—HW

For you, Alan, with love.
June 26 was a very good day—LO

GROSSET & DUNLAP
An Imprint of Penguin Random House LLC, New York

The publisher does not have any control over and does not assume any
responsibility for author or third-party websites or their content.

Text copyright © 2005 by Henry Winkler and Lin Oliver Productions, Inc.
Cover illustration by Tim Heitz, copyright © 2013 by Penguin Random House LLC.
Interior illustrations copyright © 2005 by Penguin Random House LLC.
All rights reserved. Published by Grosset & Dunlap,
an imprint of Penguin Random House LLC, New York.
GROSSET & DUNLAP is a trademark of Penguin Random House LLC.
Printed in the USA.

Visit us online at www.penguinrandomhouse.com.

Library of Congress Control Number: 2005000554

Proprietary ISBN 9781101951989   10 9 8 7 6 5 4 3 2 1

Part of Boxed Set ISBN 9781101951996

CHAPTER 1

"Disgusting!" I groaned to my sister, Emily. "Get your lizard out of the cream cheese. She's leaving claw marks."

"Blueberry cream cheese happens to be Katherine's favorite," Emily said. "She loves the berry chunks."

We were standing in the middle of the Crunchy Pickle, the deli our family owns on the Upper West Side of New York. Correction. Emily and I were standing in the middle of the deli. Katherine, Emily's pet iguana, was standing in the middle of the cream-cheese bowl. She was perched on top of one of the booth tables, snapping up cream cheese from the smoked fish platter with her long, gray, bumpy tongue. A blob of blueberry cream cheese hung off her snout. It looked like an iguana pimple.

"Reptiles are not allowed in restaurants," I said. "It's against the law."

"Says who?" Emily wanted to know.

"Says me and the entire health department of the city of New York," I answered.

Sometimes I wonder about Emily. I mean, what was she thinking, bringing Katherine here, tonight of all nights? We were having a big celebration, a party my mom throws every year that she calls "Beat the Heat with Deli Meat." It's a kick-off bash to get summer business started. The Crunchy Pickle was full of people, mostly friends and neighbors, who came to sample the food. There was barely room for all the people, let alone a cream-cheese-scarfing iguana.

"Sorry, Katherine old girl, party's over," I said, picking up the bowl of blueberry cream cheese and moving it away from her snout. Katherine hissed at me, whipping her tongue out so far that it actually touched my hand.

Help! Somebody get me a Wet One! I've been licked by lizard tongue!

Robert Upchurch, third-grade nerd and geek pal to my sister, came charging to her rescue. He's a lizard lover just like Emily. He put his bony hand on my shoulder and looked me dead in the eye. He cleared his throat before he spoke. Then he cleared it again. Then one more time to get that last little bit of gunk out. As if you couldn't tell, Robert has a major mucous problem.

"Actually, Hank, I think it's lovely that Emily invited Katherine," he said.

Did he say *lovely*? What third-grader says anything is *lovely*? Lovely is a total grandma word. Something our neighbor Mrs. Fink—who I noticed was at the buffet table doing some serious damage to the hummus dip—might say. As in "Look, Hank, what *lovely* manners your sister has" or "That little beige sweater looks so *lovely* on you."

Robert took out a Kleenex from the little pack he keeps in the pocket of his white collared shirt. I wondered what else he keeps in there.

Oh, I know. Nasal spray. Probably extra-strength.

Robert blew his nose. This was no regular blow. It was a real honker. The only good thing about it was that it required Robert to take his bony hand off my shoulder.

"Katherine is not leaving, Hank," Emily said. "This is a family celebration. And Katherine is part of our family."

"I agree," Robert chimed in.

I was going to have to set my little sister and her congested boyfriend straight.

"Number One," I said, "this is not a family celebration. This is 'Beat the Heat with Deli Meat' night, which is a business event, not a family celebration."

I don't think Katherine liked my tone of voice. She let out another nasty hiss and rolled one of her creepy eyes in my general direction.

Too bad, lady lizard. You may not like what I have to say, but it's the truth.

"And Number Two," I continued, "Katherine is not a member of our family. She is a lower life-form who can't digest cabbage."

"Actually, it's true that cabbage gives iguanas gas buildup," Robert said. "And then they eventually explode. A horrible thought."

"Thanks for the useful info, Robert," I said. "I'll remember that."

"Now you understand why I find Robert so

fascinating," Emily said, flashing Robert her ickiest smile.

Fascinating? Robots are fascinating. The Mets team statistics are fascinating. But Robert Upchurch, nose-blower and fact-spewer, is not—I repeat—NOT fascinating.

"And another reason Katherine is not a family member," I added, "is because we only happen to have humans in the Zipzer family."

"Then how did you get in?" Emily shot back. Ouch! You attack that girl's iguana and she goes for the throat.

Emily stuck her tongue out at me. I stuck out my tongue right back at her. Okay, I know it's not the most mature thing for an almost eleven-year-old guy to do. But Emily is almost ten, and I didn't notice her tongue being on a leash.

Papa Pete came up to us from behind the pastrami counter, where he had been making sandwiches. He's our grandfather, and he used to own the Crunchy Pickle. He's so nice! You want to hug him every time you see him.

Papa Pete could tell that we weren't exactly having a kissy-face brother-sister moment. It must have been our tongues sticking out that gave it away.

"What seems to be the problem, my darling grandchildren?" Papa Pete said, giving Emily's cheek a pinch with his big, plump fingers.

"Hank says Katherine can't be in here," Emily said.

"In this particular case, Hank is correct," Papa Pete said. "Animals and/or lizards are not allowed in restaurants."

My ears were having a party. You go, Papa Pete. Tell that girl a thing or two.

Emily pouted and stuck her arm out toward Katherine.

"Climb up to Mama," she said, trying to sound really pathetic. She was doing a good job of it, too.

Katherine climbed up Emily's arm, digging her little claws into Emily's pink sweater until she made it all the way up to Emily's shoulder. Emily leaned over and rubbed Katherine's snout with her cheek.

"It's okay, Kathy," she whispered in her baby voice. "I still love you."

Could you just barf? I mean, what kind of

person declares her love to a hissing lizard? My sister, that's who.

"Tell you what," Papa Pete said. "Hand Katherine to me, and I'll take her back to the apartment. Then you kids can stay here and have a good time."

Didn't I tell you Papa Pete was the greatest grandpa in the world? He was willing to leave the party just so Emily wouldn't have to. He lifted Katherine off Emily's sweater and gave her a little pat on the snout. Usually, that makes Katherine hiss, but instead she just settled into Papa Pete's big hand. Even that nasty-tempered iguana has to love Papa Pete.

"Why doesn't Emily take Katherine home herself?" I asked Papa Pete.

"Because Emily is a nine-year-old who isn't going walking by herself at night," Papa Pete said.

"It's not fair, Papa Pete. You shouldn't have to leave the party."

"Trust me, Hankie. It's my pleasure. Mrs. Fink keeps trying to feed me hummus dip. What does she think I am, a baby? I need a break."

You already know that Mrs. Fink is our next-door neighbor. But there are two other things you should know about her. One is that she has a crush on Papa Pete. The other is that she has removable teeth. Both of these facts are probably the reason that Papa Pete was willing to leave the party. As a matter of fact, he grabbed Katherine and was out the door so quickly, I thought I saw a trail of smoke coming from under his heels.

As Papa Pete raced out the door onto Broadway, he almost knocked down Frankie and Ashley, who were just running in ahead of Frankie's dad. Frankie Townsend is my best friend, and Ashley Wong is my other best friend.

"Are we too late?" Ashley asked me. She stopped to catch her breath.

"I hope we didn't miss the Invent Your Own Sandwich Contest," Frankie said. "I've got a real winner."

Frankie always seems so confident. Why shouldn't he be? Things are easy for him. Like he and Ashley are both great students, not like me who has a hard time in school.

"Check this out, Zip," Frankie said, lowering his voice to a whisper. "I'm going to start with a layer of soystrami, then a layer of pickles, soy turkey, a layer of green olives, soylami, and a layer of pimentos. On Wonder bread, with melted provolone on each slice."

"I must be really hungry," Ashley said, "because that's actually sounding good to me."

In case you aren't familiar with soystrami or soylami, they are what my mom calls "mock deli meats." My mom's mission in life is to create healthy deli luncheon meats for the twenty-first century. So she takes perfectly delicious foods like pastrami and salami and messes them up by adding stuff like soy and crushed walnuts, putting them smack in the middle of the no-taste zone.

"Wait until you hear my recipe," Ashley said. "I've got a triple decker that's going to roll your socks up and down."

But just as she opened her mouth to describe it, Dr. Townsend stood up and clinked on his glass with a spoon. Dr. Townsend, Frankie's dad, loves to make speeches and toasts. Whenever I go to dinner at their house, even if it's just a regular dinner on a Wednesday night, he clinks on a glass to get everyone's attention and then launches into one of his long toasts. He's a professor of African-American Studies at Columbia University and he's really smart, but he uses more big words in one sentence than most people use in a year. I always need Frankie to translate what he's saying.

"Ladies and gentlemen," Dr. Townsend began, having gotten the attention of everyone in the deli, "I believe we should all take this opportunity to salute the ancient ritual surrounding the summer solstice."

"Wow, that sounds like fun," I whispered to Frankie. "If only I knew what he was saying."

"Let us raise our vessels with joy and anticipation," Dr. Townsend said, "as we surrender to the season of relaxation and renewal."

"Yes! Yes!" I shouted, before I could stop myself.

It all sounded so good that it took me a second to realize I didn't have the slightest idea what I was yes-yes-ing.

"Frankie, can you translate?" I whispered.

"Sure, Zip. He said have a nice summer."

"He did? Then of course yes-yes."

"And profound gratitude to the Zipzers," Dr. Townsend continued, raising his glass toward my mom and dad, who were standing by the buffet table. My mom had some coleslaw hanging from her blond, curly hair. She always has something from the menu in her hair. My dad was wearing his glasses on the tip of his nose, like he does when he works a crossword puzzle. They both looked kind of goofy but very happy. "You have our deepest appreciation for providing this neighborhood festivity with a sumptuous feast," Dr. Townsend said.

I looked at Frankie. I didn't even have to ask for a translation.

"He said thanks for dinner."

"Yes! Yes!" I hollered. Whoops, I did it again.

That really made Ashley laugh.

"And most of all, I raise my glass to the children in the room," Dr. Townsend said, turning to us. "My congratulations on a finely executed school year. Enjoy this well-earned season of freedom as you begin your Junior Explorers Summer Program, so rife with adventure, amusement, and surprise."

Everyone in the deli started to applaud. Frankie stood up and took a bow. He loves the spotlight. Everyone applauded even louder.

"Come forward, children, so we can gaze at the bliss radiating from your faces," Dr. Townsend said.

All the kids went to stand next to Dr. Townsend. Frankie and Ashley, Robert and Emily, Ryan Shimozato and Heather Payne, who go to school with us and live in the neighborhood. We all took a bow. It was really fun.

Suddenly, I heard a voice from the back of the room, a voice that never, ever has anything nice to say. It was Nick the Tick McKelty, the meanest mouth in the entire fourth grade. I hadn't seen him come in, but his dad owns the bowling alley a few streets uptown, so I'm sure my mom and dad invited them.

"Sit down, Ziphead!" McKelty shouted. "He's not talking about you."

That McKelty. Leave it to him. I could feel my face starting to turn red.

"He's talking about us kids in the Junior Explorers Program," McKelty shouted, "not the dummies like you who have to go to summer school."

How could someone be so mean in public? I'll never, ever figure that out.

"Excuse me, Nicholas," Dr. Townsend said. "I'm wishing all the children a wonderful summer, regardless of what program they're attending."

That was nice of him to say, but it was too late. Everyone in the deli had already heard McKelty. I'm sure they were all feeling sorry for me, the dummy who has to go to summer school.

They were right. Everyone else was going to be a Junior Explorer.

Not me, though. I was going to summer school.

Stupid, boring, horrible, hideous summer school.

TEN REASONS WHY SUMMER SCHOOL STINKS MORE THAN MY GYM SOCKS

1. You can't dump summer school into a washing machine and make the stink go away.
2. Gym socks are soft and comfortable. Need I say more?
3. You can take a pair of socks off anytime you want. You have to sit in summer school from nine to three no matter what.
4. Socks come in all sizes. Summer school only comes in three sizes: tight, tighter, and cuts off the blood flow to your brain.

5. Gym socks help me play. Summer school keeps me out of the game.
6. Gym socks absorb sweat. Summer school makes it collect between my toes. That's right—a lake between my toes.
7. Gym socks are perfect for playing toe basketball. But did you ever try to slam-dunk a classroom into your wastebasket?
8. There are many uses for gym socks—dusting your computer keyboard, shining your shoes, blowing your nose. I can't think of one good use for summer school.
9. You can use gym socks to make hand puppets to entertain small children. Summer school, on the other hand, would make them hide under the couch.
10. No matter how badly my gym socks stink, trust me, summer school stinks more.

CHAPTER 3

"**I'm not getting up,**" I said, burying my face in my pillow.

"Hank, it's the first day of summer school," my dad said. "You can't be late. Remember, first impressions are . . ."

". . . everlasting," I cut in. "I know, Dad."

It's not like I'm a mind reader or anything. It's just that I've heard all my dad's sayings a lot of times so I can finish them before he does.

"Tell you what, Dad. Since it looks like I'm going to be late, I think I should just skip school today altogether."

I dove under my blue-and-white striped blanket, hoping my dad would leave my room and forget that I was there. I counted to ten. Then to twenty. My dad didn't say a word, so I figured that maybe he had left to go get some breakfast. Slowly, I edged up toward my pillow and stuck my eyes out from under the blanket.

"Boo!" my dad said, his face pressed really close to mine. He laughed really hard, like he used to do when I was little and we played peek-a-boo.

Sure, easy for him to be in a good mood. He wasn't going to have to spend most of his summer sitting inside a classroom while all his friends were outside being Junior Explorers—swimming and running and jumping and making lanyards to hold their apartment keys around their necks.

"Your mom was up very late last night, cleaning up from 'Beat the Heat with Deli Meat' evening," my dad said. "I'm letting her sleep in, so I made breakfast for you. How's that for being a good dad?"

"What kind of good dad would make his only beloved son go to summer school?"

I was hoping he'd feel guilty and tell me I didn't have to go. It didn't work. Not even close. Instead, I got the "Be Positive" lecture.

"Hank, you need to be positive about things. Why don't you try looking at your cup as half full?"

"Dad, I'm looking in my cup, and at this moment, I can't see any liquid whatsoever."

My dad pulled the covers off me and gestured toward the bathroom. I had no choice now but to get up, walk into the bathroom, and wash Mr. Sandman out of my eyes. I heard my dad's leather slippers flip-flopping on the floor, following me into the bathroom. I knew he had more lecture on the tip of his tongue, and sure enough, he waited until I was brushing my teeth so I wouldn't be able to answer.

"Maybe summer school will be a positive and fulfilling experience for you," he said.

I almost swallowed my toothbrush. With my mouth so full of toothpaste foam and bristles, all I could do was make a sound that sounded like *youf fot to fee fridding.*

"No, I'm not kidding," my dad answered.

That was weird. How did he know what I had said? I wonder if parents take a class in understanding their kids when their mouths are full of toothpaste.

"To be perfectly truthful, Hank, fourth grade was really hard for you," he went on. "I believe going to school this summer might give you a leg up on the fifth grade."

I was finished brushing my teeth, so I was all clear to say everything I wanted to say.

"But, Dad, summers were invented for kids to kick back and relax. To journey into uncharted territories of new fun."

Wow, where'd I pull that out from? Even I was impressed.

"You'll have plenty of time to relax," my dad said, obviously not as impressed with me as I was. "We're going to the Jersey Shore for a week."

"That's not until the end of August."

"Well, after school, I'll pick you up and we'll play exciting games of Scrabble Junior," my dad said, looking like he had just had the brainstorm of the year.

"We've tried that already, Dad. Remember? I can't spell."

"And there you have the reason for summer school."

Point. Set. Match. Face it, Hank. You lost this argument, hands down.

I couldn't think of another thing to say, so

I just stormed off to the kitchen to eat my breakfast.

Wouldn't you know it, it was alphabet cereal.

CHAPTER 4

"**Aloha, campers** and students alike!" Principal Leland Love was inside the main door of PS 87, all five-feet-four inches of him, wearing a Hawaiian shirt that was so big I could have used it as a tent for an overnight in the woods.

"Check out his outfit," Frankie whispered to me as we walked inside the school lobby. "Great shirt, if you're a dancing elephant."

"I just read in *Teens in the Know* that people express themselves with their clothes," Ashley said. "Obviously, he's trying to tell us something."

"That there's a short Hawaiian wrestler inside him, dying to get out," Frankie said.

"Let's hope he doesn't succeed," Ashley answered, and we all cracked up together.

Principal Love saw us laughing, but he was

clueless, as usual. He never suspects when we're laughing at him.

"Ah, laughing faces of children always make my heart burst into song," he said, slapping me on the shoulder as I tried to sneak by. And, get this. He actually started to sing.

"Aloha to Summer Fest at PS 87.
Welcome, my children,
To a little bit of heaven."

If this song was even a tiny sample of what summer school was going to be like, I was going to have to bolt for parts unknown. The only thing that stopped me was Mr. Rock's friendly face, greeting us as he jogged down the stairs to the school lobby. Mr. Rock is the music teacher at PS 87, and trust me, if you could pick any teacher in the world for your teacher, he's the one you'd pick. It's as if he knows what kids are thinking before they even think it.

Like he could see that I was thinking about how I could escape to the Central Park Zoo and spend the summer living in the monkey habitat. Hey, I love monkeys. They're so funny.

"Hi, Hank," he said. "You're in my class."

That was the first good news I had heard

all morning. Well, let's be honest. It wasn't truly *good* news like "Hey, there's an all-night kung fu movie marathon on TV tonight." After all, I still had to go to summer school. Let's just say it was just *okay* news, which is better than terrible news, if you know what I mean. Anyway, Mr. Rock could definitely see that I wasn't jumping up and down with joy.

"I promise you, Hank, summer school will not be the worst experience you've ever had on this planet or any other."

"Mr. Rock," I whispered, "I know you're trying to make me feel better, but it's not working."

Before Mr. Rock could answer me, Principal Love held up a megaphone to his mouth.

"If you're a Junior Explorer, stand to the left of the stairs. If you're in summer school, stand to the right, please."

Almost everyone went to the left of the stairs. I did too. That's because I still can't figure out my right from my left. I almost got it a couple of weeks ago when I fell during dodgeball and skinned my left knee. For a whole week, I could tell my left from my right by where the scab was. But when it healed and fell off, I was just as confused as before.

"Mr. Zipzer," I heard Principal Love saying through the megaphone, "you are to go to the RIGHT side of the stairs. The summer-school side."

Could this be any more embarrassing? Well, maybe. If Principal Love was on the top of the Empire State Building with a megaphone the size of a blimp, shouting out across the entire city: *"Hank Zipzer does not know his left from his right, and that is only one of the many reasons he has to go to summer school!"*

Yeah, that would be a little more embarrassing. But not much.

I felt like all the kids were staring at me as I slinked over to the right side of the stairs. I looked around to check out who I was standing with. There were kids from both the fourth and fifth grades at my school. I noticed they weren't exactly the school geniuses. There was Luke "I'll pick my nose at the drop of a hat" Whitman. Matthew "I'm not toilet-trained yet" Barbarosa. Salvatore "I don't like Hank Zipzer very much" Mendez. And a girl I had only seen in Mr.

Sicilian's fourth-grade class who was talking on a cell phone saying, "Okay, Nick, I'll meet you at the bowling alley." She was smiling a lovey-dovey kind of smile.

Nick? Could she be talking to Nick McKelty? His dad does own a bowling alley on 86th Street. And the only other Nick at school insists on being called Nicholas so he won't be confused with Nick the Tick.

I looked over at the kids standing on the other side of the stairs. Sure enough, there was Nick McKelty standing at the back of the crowd, clicking off his cell phone and putting it in the pocket of his jeans.

Oh, no! I was going to be in summer school with Nick McKelty's girlfriend.

Wait a minute! How could Nick McKelty get a girlfriend? Hasn't she watched him eat, with all of the food in his mouth squishing through the openings in his snaggly teeth? Hasn't she seen the size of his super humungous feet? Hasn't she gotten a whiff of his dragon breath that has actually melted the gel in my hair?

"Joelle," I heard Mr. Rock saying, "turn off your phone. No cell phones in class."

Joelle and Nick sitting in a tree,
K-i-s-s-i-n-g.

My brain flipped over in my head and spun around, throwing itself against the inside of my skull. It refused to go on with the rhyme. I could hear it yelling *"Ptueey"* like it was trying to spit out the picture of Nick and Joelle k-i-s-s-i . . . Oh, I can't go on.

"Those of you in summer school will follow Mr. Rock to Ms. Adolf's classroom on the second floor," Principal Love announced. "Those of you in the Junior Explorers Program will come with me to the Hawaiian Isles."

"We're flying to Hawaii?" Ashley asked.

"In our minds we are, Ms. Wong," Principal Love said. "Oh, the joys of imagination running wild."

"I guess my imagination is walking slow," Frankie said, "because I don't get it."

"The theme of this week's Junior Explorers Program is Passport to Hawaii, a salute to our fiftieth state," Principal Love explained. "We will be learning to hula dance, and we'll all be finding out how low we can go as we limbo the night away at Friday's Hawaiian luau extravaganza."

There was a buzz among the kids. A luau and a limbo contest. Wow, it sounded like so much fun.

"May I introduce you to your hula instructor," Principal Love said in his tall-man, sports-announcer voice. That big voice always seems so funny coming out of such a small man.

At that very moment, the hall doors to the teachers' lounge swung open and Ms. Adolf, my fourth-grade teacher, came out into the hall. She was wearing a grass skirt and a bikini top made out of two coconuts, which she wore over gray Bermuda shorts and a gray long-sleeved shirt. No, I am not kidding you. She had an entire hula-dancer outfit on *over* her regular clothes. And you're not going to believe this: The coconuts even had smiley faces on them. It was a sight that for a second made me actually grateful I had not gotten a passport to Hawaii.

"Aloha, pupils," she said, shaking her hips in a move that looked like a hippo looking for a place to pee. Ms. Adolf isn't exactly the hip-shaking type.

I glanced over at Frankie and Ashley. Frankie

was biting his lower lip really hard to keep from laughing. Ashley was actually holding her top lip over her bottom lip so she wouldn't start to giggle. Once she starts giggling, there's no stopping her.

"All you explorers follow us out to the white sand beaches of Waikiki." Principal Love pointed to the sandbox on the playground. They had propped up two huge paper palm trees there and spread beach blankets on the ground in the area around the swings.

"Those of you in summer school, follow me upstairs," Mr. Rock said.

The Junior Explorers all ran after Principal Love and headed out the doors onto the playground. The rest of us marched up the stairs and into the classroom. There were no palm trees, no beaches, no blankets.

What was there was a blackboard, chalk, and—oh, goody—brand-new erasers.

We took our seats in the classroom. Mr. Rock said we could sit anywhere we wanted, so I took a seat next to the window where I could see the Junior Explorers. They were already starting to play beach games on the playground. Boy, that was a tough sight to see. There I was, sitting at my desk looking through my backpack for a sharpened number-two pencil. And just on the other side of the glass, two floors down, were all the rest of the kids, doing the normal summer thing—having fun. If you're thinking that looking out the window at everyone else having fun put me in a bad mood, then you're a great thinker.

We were in Ms. Adolf's classroom, my old fourth-grade room. Same old pale green walls. Same old clock on the wall with the same old hands ticking soooooo slowly from one minute to the next.

There are thirty-two seats in our classroom. I know this because I spent the last year counting them every time I wasn't paying attention to Ms. Adolf, which was most of the time. It's not that I don't want to pay attention. I start every day thinking that today I'm going to pay attention from nine to three. It's just that my mind will not cooperate. By ten after nine, I'm thinking about the Mets game, and by nine-fifteen, I'm wondering if my dachshund, Cheerio, is licking the bricks over our fireplace, and by nine-sixteen, I've already gone into orbit around the outer rings of Saturn.

Anyway, back on Earth, there were a lot of empty seats in the class because there were only eleven of us lucky enough to make the summer-school cut. I wish I wasn't so good at failing. It's one of the only things that comes really easily to me—that and dental flossing. Even my dentist says I am an excellent flosser. I can get out a raspberry seed stuck between my two back molars faster than you can say the Museum of Natural History, which by the way is about five blocks from my house if you take the short way.

In spite of the fact that most of the seats in

our class were empty, Miss Joelle "I can't stop checking my cell phone" Adwin sat down in the seat right next to me.

"Hi," she said. "Do you like gymnastics?"

That was a friendly start.

"Hi," I said back. "I can do a somersault."

Maybe she's nice, even if she does like Nick the Tick.

"Somersaults are dorky," she said. "I hear you get all Ds."

Well, so much for the nice theory.

"Who told you that?" I asked, as if I didn't know.

"My boyfriend, Nick," she said. "He also said I'm much smarter than you."

My throat started to feel all funny, like it was going to close up. I needed to have a great comeback because I knew that whatever I said would be the first thing Joelle would tell Nick when she talked to him.

I opened my mouth, but nothing came out.

Hank? Why aren't you talking? Say something. Anything. Don't just sit there.

But I just sat there. I think I made a little throat noise, but it definitely didn't come out sounding like words.

"Funny, I don't see it," Joelle said, staring at me like I was some kind of screeching monkey in the zoo.

"What are you looking for?"

She was staring at my forehead. I reached up and felt around to make sure there wasn't any dried cereal stuck up there. It was just my regular forehead. So what was she staring at?

"Nick said there's something wrong with your brain, but I can't see a bump or anything."

"Don't you and Nick have anything better to talk about than my brain?" I said. "And by the way, I have learning challenges. A lot of kids do."

Luke Whitman came strolling up to us, holding something in his left hand. Or maybe it was his right hand. It was one of them. Ordinarily, I wouldn't be too curious about what he held in his hand, because you know it'd be something truly gross. But at that moment, I wanted to grab him and hug him. I would have rather talked to just about anyone than Joelle.

"Want to see my booger?" Luke asked, opening up his hand. "It's shaped like Florida."

"Oh, look, there's Disney World," I said.

Luke cracked up.

"There's more where this came from," he said.

"Come back when you get one that looks like Texas," I told him.

This time, Joelle laughed.

"You're pretty funny for a slow learner," she said to me.

"Thanks."

Hank Zipzer, did you just say thanks to that girl? For what? Hello? She called you a slow learner. You don't thank someone for that.

To my relief, Mr. Rock decided to start class at that very moment. Anything he had to say was going to be better than me talking to Joelle about my learning speed, or lack of it.

"Okay, kids, I know this isn't your first choice of a way to spend your summer," Mr. Rock began, "but I'll try my best to make this a rollicking good time for all of us. Luke, put your booger in a Kleenex and take your seat."

Mr. Rock was pretty cool. Ms. Adolf would have sent Luke to the office for walking around with a booger in his hand.

I looked out the window again. I could see Frankie on the playground, playing volley-ball with a multi-colored beach ball. He was setting for Ryan Shimozato. They were laughing. Ashley was at a crafts table, making a Hawaiian necklace out of paper flowers. I hoped they had rhinestones there for her. She glues rhinestones onto everything.

Mr. Rock asked each of us to say one word that best describes our personality, so that we'd get to know one another. Joelle said *popular*. Who was she kidding? Being liked by Nick McKelty does not make you popular. It makes you a creepette. Salvatore said *tough*. I'd say he had a point there. When it came to me, I said *Hankish*. Mr. Rock laughed out loud.

"That's very creative, Hank," he said. "We're going to have fun this summer, I can tell."

Okay, Hank, Mr. Rock thinks you're creative. He said we're going to have a rollicking good time. Give it a chance. Keep an open mind.

"Are you ready, kids? Here's the plan," Mr. Rock said. "This summer, we're going to be reviewing our math skills, which will help you this coming fall. And I've thought of a creative way to combine your reading, vocabulary, spelling, and note-taking practice."

"Wow," Luke Whitman said. "I'm shaking with excitement."

"Give me a chance, Luke," Mr. Rock said. "Wait until you hear the idea. You might actually quiver like jelly."

You're not going to believe this, but I was curious to hear his idea.

"I want you all to pick a person in history that you admire," Mr. Rock said, leaning on the edge of Ms. Adolf's desk. "On Friday, we'll all meet your famous person, when you present everything you've learned about him or her to the class." Mr. Rock seemed pretty excited about this assignment.

"Sounds like an oral report to me," Luke Whitman said.

"In a way, it is," Mr. Rock said without sounding even a little annoyed. "After all, this is school. But I hope it will be fun, too. I encourage you to be as creative as you can be. Try to become your famous person."

Wait a minute. I'm right back where I started at the beginning of fourth grade—doing a report.

I couldn't do it then. I can't do it now.

Hey, Mr. Rock. You promised a rollicking good time.

This feels like a rollicking prison sentence to me.

CHAPTER 6

I sat there at my desk, watching my leg bounce up and down like it does when I'm nervous. It was quiet time, and we were each supposed to be making a list of some famous people we'd like to report on.

I couldn't think of one.

There was George Washington, but he had wooden teeth. That's gross. There was Abraham Lincoln, but he had a mole that always reminds me of the one Principal Love has on his face. That's annoying. There was good old Thomas Edison, but he invented so many things that by the time I'd get through listing them, my report would be too long.

Wait a minute. How about Spider-Man? He's famous. Oh, I forgot. He's not real. I wish he were. Then maybe he'd help me swing out of this classroom on his webs.

Mr. Rock went around the room, asking kids what famous person they had decided on. By the time the bell rang for recess, I still hadn't come up with anyone. On my way out of class, Mr. Rock stopped me at the door.

"Well, Hank, have you made a decision?"

"Here's the problem, Mr. Rock," I said. "There are so many people to choose from, I just can't decide."

"I have six words for you, Hank," Mr. Rock said.

"You don't have to do it?" I said, hoping like crazy those were the words he was thinking of.

"You should report on Albert Einstein," he said. Not the six words I had in mind.

"Albert Einstein. Did he play for the Mets?" I asked.

"No, but he did figure out that the fastest fastball could never travel faster than the speed of light," Mr. Rock said. "Albert Einstein was the greatest genius of the twentieth century. I think you have a lot in common with him."

Me and the greatest genius of the twentieth century have something in common?

Mr. Rock, get a grip.

CHAPTER 7

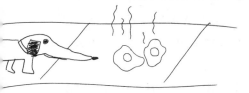

There was one good thing about summer school and that was recess. I would have included lunch, too, except that I was still nauseous at the thought of having to sit in a classroom during a summer month.

The minute Mr. Rock let me go, I bolted outside for recess. When I first hit the playground, the city sun felt great on my face. But by the time I ran across the yard, I was dripping with sweat and my Mets T-shirt was sticking to my skin. New York gets really hot in the summertime. I think it's because the buildings are so tall that they don't let the air move around.

Papa Pete always says that the sidewalk gets so hot, you could fry an egg on it. Once, when it was my turn to walk Cheerio, I took an egg from the refrigerator and tried frying it on the sidewalk. Cheerio sucked the egg up before I got a chance to see if the experiment worked. He was so happy, he tried to lick my face to say thanks, but I don't let dogs with raw-yolk mustaches lick me. I think that hurt his feelings, but I'm sure you understand my thinking.

I headed for the Hawaiian Islands, otherwise known as the area by the swings where the Junior Explorers had their camp. They were learning the limbo. You probably know this, but in case you do the limbo, it's a dance where you see how low you can go while inching yourself forward underneath a pole. Ms. Adolf was holding one side of the long bamboo pole, and Principal Love was holding the other. All the Junior Explorer kids were standing in line, waiting their turn.

I watched for a minute as Robert tried to go under the limbo pole. He kept falling down flat on his back and then looking over at Emily and laughing. Finally, he flipped over onto his stomach and slithered under the pole like a snake. He is so skinny that when he was lying flat on the sand, you almost couldn't see him. He looked like one of those bony fish that bury themselves in the sand at the bottom of the ocean.

After Robert, Frankie took his turn. He was the coolest. He didn't just get down low, he got down low with real style, shaking his shoulders one way and his hips another. *Man oh man,* I thought. *My friend Frankie is good at everything—magic, math, and even the limbo.* You should have seen him—he looked like a crab racing for the ocean. It was awesome.

"Let's hear it for Frankie Townsend," I called out to the other kids, and started clapping my hands like crazy. All the other kids joined in the applause. Everybody but Nick McKelty. He hates to see anyone but his garbage-Dumpster self get attention.

"What's so great about Townsend?" McKelty said. "Any idiot can do the limbo. Like Zipperbutt here. Let's see you do it, moron."

"As a matter of fact, Nick, I am a limbo expert," I said.

Now, between you and me, I've never done the limbo in my life, but in the heat of the moment, I couldn't stop the words from shooting out my mouth.

"It so happens that Hank could go under a toothpick with a top hat on," Ashley chimed in. She loves to give McKelty a hard time.

I shot her a look. If she could have heard my eyes, they would have been saying, "Ease up, Ashweena. I don't even know if I can do this."

I stepped up to the limbo bar. I never thought I would say this, but I was really happy to hear Ms. Adolf's voice calling out to me.

"Henry," she said, "I'm afraid that doing the limbo is out of the question for you. It is a privilege reserved for Junior Explorers only."

"That is so disappointing, Ms. Adolf," I said, not meaning a word of it.

"Don't be disappointed, Mr. Zipzer," Principal Love said. "This will give you something to strive for. Young people need a destination before they board the train of life."

"You are absolutely right, Principal Love," I said, even though I had no idea what he was talking about. You never know what Principal Love is saying. You just agree with him and sooner or later he stops talking. Usually later.

I walked away from the limbo pole.

"Too bad, loser!" McKelty shouted to me.

"Looks like you'll just have to take my turn," I said to him.

"No can do," he said. "Joelle needs me to program the speed dial on her new phone. Don't you, Joelle?"

I looked over to the side of the limbo area. Joelle was waving frantically to Nick. Her cell phone was strapped around her wrist, and as she waved, it looked like a tetherball spinning around the pole. Why did she always have her cell phone with her? Who would be calling her, anyway? Oh, I know. The Society of Girls with Disgusting Boyfriends offering her a lifetime membership. She should be president of that group.

As I walked away, I saw Joelle doing a cartwheel over to where Nick was standing. The cartwheel wasn't so great, but if they had a cell-phone Olympics, she'd get a Gold Medal hands down.

I still had fifteen minutes of recess left with not much to do. I saw Luke Whitman crawling around in the bushes, looking for slugs. He'd probably like it if I joined him, but I don't feel very at home with slimy things.

On the other side of the playground, I saw Matthew and Salvatore playing handball, and I thought maybe they'd let me in their game. I headed over there, taking a shortcut through the sandbox where the little kids play.

"Hey, you're stepping on my city," I heard a squeaky voice say.

I hadn't bothered to look down, but when I did, I saw this micro-kid drawing the Manhattan skyline in the sand with the handle of a red plastic shovel.

"What?" I said to him.

"You just destroyed the Brooklyn Bridge. See?"

"Oh, sorry, little dude. I didn't see it."

He pointed to his drawing in the sand. When I looked down at it, my eyes nearly popped out of my head. He had drawn the Empire State Building, the Chrysler Building, the Brooklyn Bridge, and even the Statue of Liberty right in the middle of the Hudson River. It was really good.

"You drew all this?" I said to the kindergartner.

"Uh-huh," he answered, shaking his head

so his red curls bounced around like they were on springs.

"And your teacher didn't help you?"

"Nope. I did it all by myself. And now I have to do the bridge over again."

"Can I help you?"

He handed me a blue plastic shovel.

"You can make a tugboat on the river."

"I've never drawn a tugboat before. I'm not sure I know how."

"It's easy," he said.

"Just because it's easy for you doesn't mean it's easy for me. Maybe I'll just sit here and watch you draw. Is that okay?"

"Yup."

"What's your name?" I asked him. He stuck his tongue out of the side of his mouth while he drew. I do that sometimes when I'm concentrating.

"Mason Harris Jerome Dunn."

"My name's Hank."

"Oh."

"Are you going to pre-kindergarten, Mason?"

"I'm a Bobcat."

"I was a Bobcat, too, before I went to kindergarten."

"Did you like to finger paint? Because I think it's fun."

I tried to remember back to the summer before I started kindergarten, when I went to the Bobcat summer program at PS 87. It seemed like so long ago—when school was still fun.

Mason went on drawing while I watched. Suddenly, from behind me came the booming voice of a Gila monster. I could smell the bad breath heading my way. I think I even saw Mason Harris Jerome Dunn's nose twitch. Poor little nose. It was so new to the world, I'm sure it had never smelled anything like McKelty's mud breath.

"Well, look who found a friend!" McKelty smirked, kicking up some sand with his size-twelve feet. "Finally came up with someone who knows less than you do, huh, Zipper Face?"

"I don't like him," whispered Mason.

"I'm with you, dude," I whispered back.

McKelty took a giant step forward into the sandbox and looked down at Mason's drawing.

"What's that supposed to be?"

Mason didn't answer him, just went on drawing.

"It looks like scribble scrabble," McKelty said.

"McKelty, sometimes you just amaze me," I said. "Anybody with eyes can see it's New York. Why don't you leave the kid alone?"

"No problem," McKelty said. "Unlike some people I know, I have kids my own age to play with."

He ran over to the handball court, kicking up more sand as he left. I noticed that when he reached the court, Salvatore and Matthew stopped mid-game, dropped the ball, and left. So much for McKelty having friends to play with.

I turned to Mason. He had put down his red shovel. He looked sad.

"Hey, dude, why'd you stop drawing?"

"That mean boy called it scribble scrabble."

"Are you kidding? He doesn't know what he's talking about. This is great art."

The recess bell rang.

"Listen, little dude," I said, "I got to go. Maybe I'll see you again, okay?"

Mason didn't answer. As I walked off, I turned around to look at him. I saw him pick up his red shovel and start to repair the part of the Brooklyn Bridge that I had stomped on.

That a boy, Mason. Don't let anyone stop you.

CHAPTER 8

As we walked home after school, I told Frankie and Ashley about Mason. We agreed that kindergartners are way up there on the cute scale along with puppies and baby pandas. By the time we got to Mr. Kim's grocery store, where he was putting fresh water in each of the buckets of pink tulips, we had made a list of the cutest things about kindergartners.

See if you can figure out whose reason is whose. I'll bet you can.

THE TEN CUTEST THINGS ABOUT
KINDERGARTNERS
By Hank, Ashley, and Frankie

1. They have puffy cheeks.
2. They have the cutest little voices and the cutest little fingernails.

3. Every time you do a magic trick, they say, "Woweeeee."
4. Their sneakers are so small, they look like toys.
5. They like it when you help them.
6. They love sparkly things like rhinestones.
7. They say funny things like "buffalo" instead of "beautiful."
8. They're so light that when you pick them up, you feel strong.
9. They don't make fun of you if you can't read.
10. They look up to fourth-graders.

ANSWER GUIDE: 1. Ashley, 2. Ashley, 3. Frankie, 4. Ashley, 5. Hank, 6. Ashley (that's an easy one), 7. Hank, 8. Frankie, 9. Hank (another easy one), 10. All three of us

CHAPTER 9

Dinner at my house that night was really obnoxious. Well, the actual dinner—as in the tofu tacos and Spanish rice—wasn't horrible. At least, it wasn't as bad as the cauliflower-raisin-garlic soup my mom had brewed up a couple of nights before. But the company and the conversation stunk up the dinner big time.

Emily had the bright idea to invite Robert over for dinner. His mother designs pop-up greeting cards, and she had to go to an important meeting for all the pop-up designers in New York. I imagine they probably need to meet a lot because making pop-up cards seems like a really hard thing to do. You know the card that's a giant birthday cake with a candle on top and when you open it up, the whole cake jumps out at you? I've always wondered how they get it to do that. I don't think I could ever be a pop-up card maker. You have to be so exact. I'm not very good with details. I keep losing them all the time.

Anyway, Robert came to dinner and brought his new pet, a gecko that he had named Bruce. If I had a gecko—which I wouldn't, because I'm not a fan of pets with scaly skin—but if I did, I'd name it something cool like Fang or Spike. Only someone like Robert, who wears a white shirt and tie to school every day, would name his pet gecko Bruce.

As we sat down at the table to eat, I noticed that Katherine wasn't there. She usually sits on Emily's shoulder during dinner, hissing at her own reflection in the saltshaker and snatching carrots off our plates with her tongue. Emily said Katherine didn't come to dinner because she was feeling a little under the weather, but I'm sure the old lizard was just jealous of Bruce. She isn't the type who'd want to share her mini-carrots with another reptile.

Bruce was sitting in a plastic box on the table between Robert and Emily. Or at least I think he was in it, because when you looked inside the box, all you could see were leaves and rocks and a water dish. Correction. A water thingamajiggy. That was no dish.

"Hey, Robert, what exactly is that thingamajiggy holding your gecko's water?"

"That happens to be the cap for the cream I use to moisten the dry skin in my ears," he answered.

"Too much information, Robert. I'm getting nauseous."

"I think it's a very inventive use of an ear-cream container," Emily said. "Reuse and recycle, that's what I say."

Don't get me wrong. I'm all for recycling. It was the dry-skin-in-the-ears part that got my stomach churning. I couldn't believe Robert and Emily were actually discussing ear moistening cream at our family dinner table. I tell you, they are two peas in a freaky, geeky pod. And my parents just sat there through the whole conversation, like we were talking about something normal.

"By the way, Robert, where exactly is Bruce?" I asked, trying to find him inside the plastic container.

"That's him," Robert said.

I studied the box. To me, it looked gecko-less.

"Come on, this thing is empty," I said. "Stop kidding around."

"He's right there, Hank," Emily said. "Isn't he one gorgeous gecko?"

I looked in the container and noticed a little gray thing sticking out from under the wilted lettuce leaf on the bottom of the box.

"That's him? I thought it was a pebble."

"For your information, rocks do not have eyes," Emily said. "At least, not the rocks I know."

She and Robert started to laugh, snorting in and out like a couple of rhinos with colds.

"So sue me," I said. "I thought you took a magic marker and put two dots on a rock."

"Hank, watch your tone of voice," my mom said, shooting me the watch-your-tone-of-voice look that moms are so good at. Then she changed the subject, another mom specialty.

"So, how was everyone's day?" she asked cheerfully.

"Junior Explorers is so fun. Isn't it, Robert?" Emily said.

"Mrs. Zipzer, I was a total crack-up today," Robert chimed in.

"I can't wait to hear this," I said. "Please, Robert. Share it all."

"Hank, what's your problem?" My dad raised one eyebrow at me, a thing he does when he's not mad yet but is just about to be. "Robert is our guest."

I knew I was being grouchy, but I couldn't help myself. It was really hard to hear about their fun time in Junior Explorers, while all I did was watch it through my classroom window. I took a bite of my tofu taco and prepared to chew it really hard, then realized I didn't have to. My mom's tofu was soft and mushy.

"We learned the hula and the limbo," Emily went on.

"I kept falling over backward under the limbo rod, so finally I got on my stomach and crawled under the bar like a salamander." Robert started to laugh at the memory.

Emily burst out laughing, too. "You should have seen him. He was a perfect salamander."

The two of them held their sides, and their

snorty rhino laughter made a second appearance at the table.

I wish I could crawl into that box and hang out with Bruce under the wilted lettuce leaf. Hey, I like salad.

"And guess what?" Emily said when she finally got control of herself. "This Friday we're having a luau extravaganza and a sleepover under the stars. Doesn't that sound so *magnifico*?"

"You guys get to sleep out on the playground?" I could hardly believe my ears. "Frankie and Ashley never told me that."

"They probably didn't want to make you feel bad," my dad said.

"Well, I do anyway."

"I'll tell you all about it, Hank," Robert said. "In fact, I'll even write down what each person does in the talent show."

"There's a talent show, too?" This was almost too much for me.

Robert nodded.

"Robert and I are entering," Emily said. "We're going to train Bruce to do his own version of the hula, and we're making a hula skirt for him out of wheatgrass."

"Oh, wheatgrass is so healthy," my mom said. "Of course, that's when you swallow it. I don't know if there are healthy benefits for wearing it."

"The great thing is, he's so little that we only need four blades of grass," Robert added.

"Congratulations," I said. "You'll probably get in the Guinness Book of World Records for making the smallest hula skirt in history."

"Great idea, Hank," Robert said. "We'll have to take a picture of Bruce in his skirt and submit it to them."

"News flash, Robert. I was kidding. As in joke."

"Oh, right," Robert said. "Smallest hula skirt in history. Pretty funny, huh, Emily?"

He and my sister hauled out their rhino snorts for the third time that night.

"What are the other children doing for the talent show?" my mom asked as she reached for another tofu taco. She likes her own cooking, which is an excellent thing because no one else in the family does.

"Heather Payne is going to sing 'Home on

the Range,' and Frankie and Ashley are doing a magic trick," Emily said.

That did it! I dropped my tofu taco in my lap. Cheerio jumped up on his two back legs and gulped it down like the doggy vacuum cleaner he is.

"Frankie and Ashley are doing a magic trick?" I confess, I was practically crying. "That's not fair! They can't do magic without me. Our act is called Magik 3, not Magik 2."

Frankie, Ashley, and I have a magic act. True, we hadn't performed in a while, not since my twin cousins' birthday party, when we made a bunch of three-year-olds cry by making their M&Ms disappear. But still, we're all part of Magik 3. And Frankie always says I'm the best magician's assistant he's ever had. I couldn't believe he would perform without me. I just couldn't believe it.

"I saw their names written down on the sign-up sheet," Emily said. "It said *An Island Magic Trick by Frankie Townsend with the assistance of Miss Ashley Wong.*"

"That does it! I'm going to the luau, too," I declared right then and there. "We'll just add my name to the sign-up sheet. Do we have to bring our own sleeping bags?"

"Not so fast, young man," my dad piped up, swallowing a mouthful of Spanish rice. "This is a privilege you haven't earned yet."

"But, Dad, they're getting to have so much fun. And all I get to do is a stupid report on a famous person I admire."

"That sounds most interesting, Hank."

"Oh, right! Mr. Rock tells me I should do a report on Albert Einstein, and I don't even have a clue who this guy is, so how can it be interesting to admire someone you don't even know?"

"Albert Einstein discovered the theory of relativity," Robert the walking encyclopedia spewed out. "I'm so sorry I never got to discuss that with him in person."

"I'll find out where he lives and you can go visit him," I snapped.

"He's dead," Emily said.

"I knew that."

I got up from the table and headed for my room without even asking to be excused. I didn't need to be corrected by my little sister in front of Robert the Bony and Bruce the Invisible Gecko.

"Stanley," my mom said, "don't you think if Hank shows us he's really trying, we could consider letting him attend the luau? I mean, he does try as hard as he can."

I stopped dead in my tracks. Mothers. They can be so great, especially mine.

There was a long silence as my dad thought about her suggestion.

"Well, Randi," he said at last, "I suppose we could consider it."

Now is the time to strike, Hankster! Beg if you have to.

"I'll do anything, Dad. Anything. Just tell me what."

"If you bring me a good grade on your Albert Einstein report, I'll let you go to the luau," my dad said.

"How good? Like a C-plus good?"

He shook his head.

"B-minus?"

He shook it again.

"I think you're capable of getting an A," he said.

That taco must have gone to his head and clogged up his memory.

"It's me, Dad. Hank. The not-A student. The not-even-B student. The C student if I'm really lucky and the teacher's in a good mood, but mostly the D student. Do you know how hard it would be for me to get an A?"

"You have to reach for the stars, young man. That's the only way you'll achieve. I want to make sure you live up to your potential."

My dad pushed his chair back and put his napkin on the table. Something told me that this conversation was ending, whether I liked it or not.

An A on my report. Could I do it?

I had to. There was no way I was going to let that talent show happen without me.

Okay, Mister Albert Einstein. It's you and me. We're going all the way to the luau.

Just one question: Who the heck are you?

CHAPTER 10

Right after dinner, I called Frankie.

"Meet me in the clubhouse in five minutes," I said. "And bring Ashweena."

"I'm all over it," Frankie said.

I took the elevator to the basement and walked down the hall as fast as I could to our clubhouse, which is through the second door on the right. Wait a minute. Did I say the second door on the right? Yes, I did. And guess what? It truly is the second door on the right! This is amazing. I, who don't know my right from my left, just told you how to get to our clubhouse. I'll see you there!

I was the first to arrive. I reached around the door and switched on the light before going in. It can get a little weird in there, because it's where everyone in our apartment building stores their stuff. A couple weeks ago, I forgot to turn on the light before I went in, and I nearly jumped out of my sneakers! There were two creepy red eyes glowing at me from behind the couch. With the light on, I realized it was the same old stuffed moose head that has been hanging there as long as I can remember. Welcome to Hank's brain. Sometimes it doesn't remember what it already knows.

While I was waiting in the clubhouse for Frankie and Ashley, I started pacing around in a circle like I do when I'm working on a problem. I paced double fast, because I had two problems to work out. First, there was good old Einstein, whoever he is. And then there was the going to the luau disaster—or should I say, the NOT going to the luau disaster.

It's a good thing Frankie and Ashley arrived right away, or I would have worn a hole in the concrete floor.

"Talk to me, Zip," Frankie said, coming in and flopping down on Mrs. Park's old couch with the stuffing coming out of the arms. "What's wrong?"

"What makes you think something's wrong?"

"You're doing the circle walk," Ashley said. "You don't do the circle walk when nothing's wrong."

I opened my mouth and it all came pouring out like ketchup when you've tapped too hard on the bottom of the bottle.

"Okay, first I have to do a report on Albert Einstein, whoever he is. And if I don't get an A, I can't go to the luau, which would totally suck because—were you guys really not going to invite me to be part of the Magik 3 trick at the talent show?"

Frankie got up from the couch and grabbed me by the shoulders.

"Zip, I want you to take your arms, put them around you, and hold on to yourself," he said. "You're freaking out."

"But you guys didn't tell me there was a talent show."

"Okay, maybe that was wrong," Frankie said. "We should have told you."

"And how come you didn't invite me?"

"You're always invited," he said. "That's why it's called Magik 3, dumbo."

An instant silence fell over the room. The only

thing you could hear was the swish-swishing of the washing machine in the laundry room down the hall. Ashley shot Frankie a look, and he understood immediately.

"I take back the dumbo part," he said. "You're not dumb, my man. It's just an expression. I lost my head."

I really knew Frankie didn't mean to call me dumb, but if you're a guy like me who's always at the bottom of the class, and you feel bad about yourself sometimes, you do get extra sensitive. Know what I mean? Good. Frankie does too.

"So if I'm part of Magik 3, how come we walked all the way home from school together and no one mentioned a talent show?" I asked.

"We didn't want to rub it in," Ashley said. "Because we didn't know if you could come or not. The talent show is supposed to be just for Junior Explorers."

"But we don't care about that lame rule, right?" Frankie said. "We're Magik 3. I say we just give Principal Love the word that we can't do the act without you. And *zengawii*, you're there. No problemo."

I felt better. Until I felt worse. I had forgotten about my father.

"Whoops, problemo," I said. "The cross-word-puzzle whiz who runs my life says I can't go unless I get an A on my Einstein report."

"Ouch," Frankie said. "Yup, that sounds like Stan the Man."

"There's only one solution, Hank," Ashley said, twirling her ponytail around her index finger like she does when she's thinking up a plan. "You'll just have to get an A."

"If I could just point out one tiny, itsy-bitsy wrinkle," I said. "The last A I got was in Plays Well with Others While Building Fire Trucks with Blocks."

"Congratulations, man," Frankie said, giving me a high five. "Fire trucks are cool."

"Frankie, I was three."

"In that case, you're due for an A," Ashley said.

"Case closed," Frankie said.

He stepped over to the light switch and flipped it up and down. The lights flickered like crazy.

"Lady and gentlemen," he said, "it's the Magic Hour."

Frankie is a terrific magician. Not only does he do the tricks really well, but he has a great flair for drama. Like flipping the lights on and off. Most guys would have just said, "It's time to plan our magic act." But not Frankie Townsend. For him, it had to be Magic Hour.

"I have a concept for our act," he whispered, pulling us in close. "Zip, I am going to transform you into the ancient Hawaiian king Kahuna Huna."

"This is so cool," Ashley said. "I love Hawaiian themes."

"And you," Frankie said, pointing to Ashley, "will be Princess Leilani."

"I can see it now. I'll cover my costume with blue and green rhinestones like the ocean!"

"And for our trick, I am going to make King Kahuna Huna here appear out of the smoke from a steaming volcano."

"Can you do that?"

"*Zengawii,*" Frankie said. "Behold."

He went to the light switch and flicked it up and down again. For a minute, it looked like there was lightning in the room.

"Travel with me now to the ancient islands of Hawaii . . ." Frankie said in his magician's voice, ". . . when volcanoes breathed fire and palm trees swayed in the tropical breeze caused by those volcanoes."

Man, he was into this.

Frankie grabbed a plastic potted plant that was buried under some moldy drapes on one of the storeroom shelves. He waved it around under my nose.

"Oh great Kahuna Huna, can you smell the perfume of the sweet tropical flowers?" he said.

"Ah-choo," I sneezed, spraying dust from the plastic plant all over Frankie's hand. That thing couldn't have been dustier. I hate to think what would have happened if Robert had been here, with his horrible allergies. He would have blown us all to Fiji and back.

Frankie was rummaging around the storeroom shelves, looking for more props.

"Can you hear the magical sounds of Hawaiian strings, strumming to the rhythm of the ocean waves?" he said as he pulled something from a box on one of the shelves.

Frankie held up a toy ukulele he had found in the box. I knew that ukulele. Mrs. Fink gave it to Emily and me when she returned from the cruise to the Hawaiian islands that she took for her sixty-fifth birthday. I could never play it, but Emily had learned a couple of chords until she got bored with it and started taking flute lessons. Wow, I didn't know it wound up in the storeroom.

"Princess Leilani," Frankie said to Ashley as he handed her the ukulele, "strum to the rhythm of the ocean waves."

Ashley grabbed the ukulele and to my total surprise, started strumming it and singing some weird Hawaiian song that went: *"Oh we're going to a hooky lau. A hooky, hooky, hooky, hooky, hooky lau."* Where in the world had she learned that crazy song? Oh well, at least her singing covered up her ukulele strumming, which was pretty scary.

Frankie dug around in the boxes some more, pulling out all kinds of strange stuff.

"Come here, Kahuna Huna, and I will transform you into a king," he said to me.

I stood in front of him and he put together a

costume that would make your eyes spin around in your head. I'm not sure if that's good or bad, but I wasn't sure if my costume was good or bad, either. It was different, I'll say that much.

Frankie wrapped the flowered drapes around my head to make a headdress and then fastened it with a sparkly Christmas decoration that looked like a green, glittery pear. We pulled my shirt off, because what kind of ancient Hawaiian king would wear a Michael Jordan shirt with the words "Stuff It!" on the back? On my upper arms, the part where big muscles would have been if I had big muscles, we tied Emily's old purple soccer socks and attached some dangling toy boats made of LEGOs. Frankie said they tied in with the ocean theme.

"We need something for his feet," Ashley said. "The sneakers aren't cutting it."

Frankie poked around toward the back of the shelves. He dragged out a box that was labeled "Mrs. Eleanor Fink." Inside were two square pillows made of green velvet with gold tassels hanging from each corner.

"Take off your shoes and socks," he told me. He pulled the pillows from the box and tied each one to my feet using shoelaces from his own old soccer shoes. Once the pillows were on my feet, I tried walking a few steps. Okay, it felt good. Trust me, if you ever try walking on pillows, I think you'll find it a pretty bouncy situation.

"King Kahuna Huna walks on lava," Frankie said, "yet his feet feel no pain. Appear, oh great Kahuna Huna—and make us believe in you!"

I don't know what got in to me. Maybe it was the bouncy feet. That's a definite possibility. Or maybe it was the glittery pear hanging from my flowered headdress. That's less likely but still possible. Or maybe it was Ashley strumming the ukulele and singing, *"Oh we're going to a hooky lau."* Yes, that's probably it. But all I can tell you is that right there in our clubhouse, I started to do a hula warrior dance.

I'm talking mega hula. My hips and butt and shoulders were swaying like no ancient Hawaiian king you've ever seen.

"You go, Kahuna Huna!" Frankie shouted. "This stuff is going to knock 'em dead at the talent show."

Suddenly, I noticed that Frankie had stopped laughing and Ashley had stopped singing. They were staring at something behind me.

It was then that I realized we were not alone.

I turned around to see Mrs. Fink standing in the doorway. She was wearing her big pink bathrobe and a pink hairnet to match. What she wasn't wearing were her teeth. I know that because her mouth was hanging open and I could see her pink gummy gums. I can't really blame her. If I were looking at me with my head wrapped in her flowered drapes and my feet strapped to her green pillows, my mouth would hang open, too.

"Mrs. Fink, I can explain," I said.

"Hankie, what's to explain? You can hula!" She grinned.

Before I could say King Kahuna Huna, she grabbed me in her arms and started to dance. I could feel every part of her shake as she swiveled her hips and rotated her knees.

"Mrs. Fink!" I said, but no one could hear me because my head was buried somewhere deep in her—how can I say this?—chesty area.

I wanted to call for help, but who do you call in a situation like that? The hula police?

So instead I just kept on dancing.

Ashley started up her song again. Frankie launched into a Hawaiian-sounding magic chant. And Mrs. Fink shook like a bowl full of strawberry Jell-O.

I ask you: Where are the talent show judges when you need them?

CHAPTER 11

"**Guess what, Mr. Rock?**" I said as I walked into class the next morning. "I've decided to do my report on Albert Einstein."

"That's great, Hank. I'm glad to see you're so excited about this project."

"Not only am I excited," I said, "I've decided to get an A."

"Making that decision is the first step," Mr. Rock said. "A positive attitude can take you all the way to your goal."

As I slid into my desk, I actually believed that I could do it. The night before, I had called Papa Pete to see if he knew anything about Albert Einstein. He said he knew a few things, but he was going to pick me up after school and take me to a place where I could find out everything I needed to know. I begged him to tell me where, but he said it was a surprise. Papa Pete loves surprises. I do too. I think I get that from him.

I really, really, really wanted that A. It was the only way my dad was going to let me go to the luau and be in the talent show. And after our rehearsal in the clubhouse, I knew that our act was going to win for sure. I mean, let's be honest. Who would you vote for? King Kahuna Huna magically appearing from the smoke of a volcano and doing the meanest hula this side of Pittsburgh or Bruce the Gecko twitching his scaly tail while sitting in my sister Emily's scaly hand?

Come on, it's a no brainer.

As I opened my notebook and got out my pencils, I glanced across the aisle at Joelle. She was all hunched over in her chair, holding her cell phone to her ear. Even though she was talking softly, I could hear her.

"He thinks he's going to get an A," she was giggling into the phone. "Can you believe he actually said that?"

Was she talking about me?

"I don't know," she whispered into the phone. "Some jerk named Alfred Ein-something."

She WAS talking about me! But to who? Oh no, I bet it was Nick the Tick.

I looked out the window onto the playground. I could see the Junior Explorers bringing buckets of water over to the sandbox. Frankie had said they were going to have a sand-castle building contest. One Junior Explorer with a huge head and huger feet was standing off to one side, hunched over a cell phone. That's right. It was the one and only Nick McKelty Pest.

If you can give me ten good reasons why Joelle Adwin and Nick McKelty have to talk on the phone about what grade I might or might not get on my Albert Einstein report, I will personally come over to your house and pour you a big bowl of Froot Loops.

"Don't you have anything better to talk about?" I whispered to Joelle.

"We're not talking about you," she said.

"Right, and my name is Bernice."

I know, that's Frankie's line. He says it all the time. But since Joelle didn't really know him, and it was such a perfect comeback, I decided Frankie wouldn't mind if I borrowed it.

"Joelle, hand me your telephone now, please."

It was Mr. Rock, standing in the aisle between us. He held out his hand and waited. Joelle flipped the phone closed but didn't give it to him.

"It's mine," she said. "I need it for emergencies."

"It doesn't belong in school. I'll give it back after class."

"But, Mr. Rock," she whined, "I can't live without it."

"I promise you, Joelle," Mr. Rock said, taking the phone from her. "You'll live."

"My uncle dropped his cell phone in the toilet and flushed it away by accident," Luke Whitman said. "And he's still living."

Everyone in the class cracked up but Joelle. Her face got red, all the way to the tips of her ears. Even the freckles on her nose went from light brown to red. She was steaming mad. I knew Nick McKelty was going to be hearing about this at recess.

And he did, all right.

As I stood outside on the playground eating my 100 percent organic whole oat granola with roasted pecans bar, I could see Joelle across the playground blabbering away to Nick, hopping around like she had ants in her pants. After a long time of her blabbering, she shut up and he started blabbering back to her.

I wonder how she stands his fire-breathing badddd breath. I guess her nose is on permanent vacation.

I was wondering where my nose would go on vacation if it could pick anyplace in the world when a little voice interrupted my thoughts.

"Hi, Hank."

"Mason Harris Jerome Dunn," I said, giving a high five to the little dude. Actually, it was more of a low five. "Nice to see you, buddy."

"If we're going to be friends, can you just call me Mason?"

"It's a deal. Mason it is."

"Do you want to play at my house after school? We have Pop-Tarts."

"Hey, I'd love to, bud. I mean Mason. But today I'm going somewhere with my grandpa."

"Oh," he said.

"But I'll come over another day," I told him. "That's a fantastic idea."

"Oh," he said again.

Then from out of nowhere he gave me a hug, just like that.

Okay! That's the eleventh great thing about kindergartners. They'll hug you for no reason, just because they feel like it. How great does that feel?

I looked over at Joelle and McKelty. They were standing across the playground, looking at us.

You guessed it. They were laughing at me, probably saying how dorky it was to play with a kindergartner. And you know what I thought?

Too bad. It's their loss.

CHAPTER 12

Papa Pete came to pick me up after school. He was wearing a Mets baseball cap to keep the hot summer sun off his face, and holding a plastic bag of pickles for our snack.

I sprinted out of the main door as soon as I saw him. "Where are we going?" I asked.

"You'll see, Hankie," he said. "Have a pickle. They're very refreshing."

Papa Pete thinks many things are very refreshing. A dip in the ocean. A deep breath. A cool shower. Orange sherbet. Iced tea. A washcloth on the back of your neck. And I must say, I love everything that he thinks is refreshing.

I took a pickle from the bag and handed the other one to Papa Pete along with a paper napkin to wrap the bottom of the pickle in. My mouth was watering as I took the first bite. There's nothing like a garlic dill to make you forget that you just spent the day in summer school. As it turned out, this one was extremely juicy, which I wasn't expecting. Pickle juice squirted out of my mouth, shot up in the air, and landed with a big splat right in the center of my T-shirt.

"Oops," I said. "Now I'm going to smell like pickle for the rest of the day."

"Then you're in the right company," Papa Pete said, "because I happen to find pickle juice to be a very delicious scent."

We headed over to Broadway and 79th Street and walked down a flight of stairs into the subway station. A man with a beard was playing "Jingle Bells" on the saxophone. We listened to him while we were waiting for the train.

"Isn't he a little early for Christmas?" I whispered to Papa Pete.

"You've got to play what's in your head," Papa Pete whispered back to me as the train pulled up. He wished the man happy holidays and dropped a dollar into his saxophone case as we boarded the subway car.

It was really crowded inside, and since there wasn't any place to sit, Papa Pete and I stood up and hung onto a metal pole as the train sped downtown. He's really good at riding the subway standing up. I always try to keep my balance without holding on. It's like surfing—only underground in the city. Most of the time, I do lose my balance and go crashing into the people standing around me. Maybe Papa Pete enjoys the smell of pickle juice, but I'm pretty sure everyone smushed up against me in the subway didn't. I noticed that the space around me kept getting bigger and bigger as the other subway riders edged away.

We got off at 42nd Street and took the shuttle to Grand Central Station, which is right in the middle of midtown Manhattan. If you ever get to New York City, you really should go there. Papa Pete says the main terminal, where the ceiling looks like the sky, was at one time the biggest room in all of America. I believe him. I don't think I could run from one end to the other without having to stop and rest.

I still couldn't guess where we were going. As we walked out of the terminal and headed over to Fifth Avenue, I asked Papa Pete to give me a hint.

"It's a place I used to go to when I was your age," Papa Pete said.

Wow, that means it had been there for a really long time.

"Ray's Pizza," I guessed, knowing how much Papa Pete loves pizza.

Papa Pete shook his head. He gave me one more hint.

"The things inside can't be judged by their covers," Papa Pete said.

"Books!" I said. "You can't judge a book by its cover."

"Oh, are you a smart kid, Hankie," Papa Pete said. He may be the only person in the world who thinks so.

"I know!" I said. "We're going to a bookstore to buy a book on Albert Einstein!"

By then, we had reached the corner of Fifth Avenue and 42nd Street. Papa Pete stopped and pointed to a huge building that stretched along the entire block. There were giant columns all along the front, and two humongous stone lions guarding the entrance.

"This looks like a really important building," I said.

"It is, Hankie," Papa Pete answered. "This is the New York Public Library's main branch."

He said the words like he was saying something wonderful, such as "This is Disneyland, Hankie" or "This is Shea Stadium." I watched Papa Pete as he looked at the library. He seemed really happy to be there. Then he turned to me.

"Grandson of mine, I think it's time," Papa Pete said, giving my cheek a pinch.

"For what?" I asked.

"It's time to get you a library card."

I had gotten a library card once when I was in kindergarten and Mrs. McMurray took our class to our local branch. But of course I lost it the same day. What do you expect? It's me, Hank.

This is going to sound really weird, but Papa Pete and I had a totally great time in the library. I know you're probably thinking there's nothing cool about a library. But trust me, this one was.

First of all, it was actually cool in there. I was dripping with sweat from the hot air in the subway and the walk down Fifth Avenue. But inside the library, the air was very refreshing, as Papa Pete would say.

After we went inside, we walked up a long marble staircase, like the kind they built for kings and queens in England. Upstairs, we found a giant room that was lined with books on all sides. Huge chandeliers hung from the ceiling. About a million computer monitors sat on long wooden tables, glowing like those strange fish that live in the darkest part of the ocean. It was the kind of place that makes you feel like you want to whisper, which is a good feeling to have, because it's a library rule. There are signs everywhere that say "Sssshhhhh."

Papa Pete went up to the front desk and told them I wanted to check out some books. A really nice woman named Mrs. Patron told us that we couldn't check out books at this branch. This branch was only for research. *Oh, well,* I thought, *I could survive another few years without a library card.* Wrong. Mrs. Patron directed us across the street to the lending library. There, another nice woman helped me fill out some forms. Then she went into a back room and was gone for a while. When she came out, she handed me my very own library card.

Henry Daniel Zipzer, it said.

It didn't say whether or not I was a good reader. It didn't say whether or not I had learning challenges. All it said was that I was a person who wanted to check out books from the library.

If you ask me, that is pretty darn cool.

CHAPTER 13

Papa Pete and I walked around the library. We ended up checking out six books on Albert Einstein. I looked for the ones that weren't too thick and that had a lot of pictures inside. The librarian said it was okay to get books with a lot of pictures and even suggested books on tape. She said the most important thing was to enjoy the books. I don't think Ms. Adolf would agree with that! She thinks that listening to a book on tape is cheating. I know it's not. When I did my report on the Hopi Indians, I learned everything about them from a book on tape, and I got a really good grade. So there, Ms. Adolf! Get with it.

After we left the library, we stopped for hot dogs with brown mustard and grilled onions from Papa Pete's favorite cart. Then we got back on the subway and arrived at my apartment just as my mom was putting dinner on the table. Papa Pete pointed to his eyeballs and told her we were full up to here with pickles and hot dogs, which meant we didn't have to eat her Beet Surprise Soufflé. As far as I'm concerned, the only thing surprising about beets is how bad they taste and how red they make your tongue.

While the others were eating, Papa Pete and I went into my bedroom and started reading up on Einstein. We spread the books out all over the floor, and I flopped from one to the other, looking at the pictures and reading what I could. Papa Pete read me the words I couldn't sound out. There were plenty of those, believe me.

At first, I couldn't figure out why Mr. Rock thought I would be so interested in Albert Einstein. First of all, he had this really crazy head of gray hair that stuck out all over. It looked like he had rubbed a balloon over it so that it was filled with static electricity. Add to that a big, bushy mustache that covered half his face. Then add to that the fact that the scientific theories he developed were really hard to under-stand. They were all about the universe and gravity and time and space. Oh, and the speed of light. The only thing I know about the speed of light is that Superman flies faster than it.

But as we continued to look through the books, I discovered two really interesting things about old Albert.

The first was that when he was a kid, he didn't get such great grades in school. For a long time, people thought he might even have had dyslexia, which is the name for the learning challenge that I have. These days, they're pretty sure that he didn't actually have dyslexia, but one thing is for sure: He got really bored in school and didn't do nearly as well as he should have. And get this, he was especially slow in reading. Hey, my middle name should be Albert.

"Albert Einstein was an underachiever, like me," I told Papa Pete, rolling over onto my back. "How about that?"

Papa Pete picked up the book I was reading. It had a quotation from old Al himself that he read aloud to me.

"*I have no special talents,*" Papa Pete read. "*I am only passionately curious.*"

"Hey, I'm curious too," I said. "That's why I'm always wondering about stuff."

The second really interesting thing I found out about old Albert was that he had a great imagination. In fact, he won a humongous science award called the Nobel Prize for discovering that light always travels at a constant speed, which is 186,000 miles per second. But here's the really cool part: The thing that helped him develop his theory about the speed of light was that he imagined himself riding on a beam of light, going that fast.

Papa Pete turned the page of his book and read another quote from Einstein.

"Imagination is more important than knowledge," he said.

Oh yes, I couldn't agree more. I'm down with that, as Frankie would say. I love to use my imagination. And I'm pretty good at it, too. Even Mr. Rock said so.

"You know what, Papa Pete?" I said. "I like everything about this Albert Einstein guy. Except his hairdo."

Papa Pete smiled. "He was a great man," he said. "Do you know he didn't believe in war? That's a very refreshing thought."

I look at it this way. Any grown-up who

spends his time wondering what would happen if he went cruising around the universe on a beam of light has to be my kind of guy.

CHAPTER 14

Frankie and Ashley came over after dinner. I thought they were just stopping in to see Papa Pete. They love it when he pinches their cheeks and calls them his grandkids, too. But it turned out that they had more on their minds.

"Frankie and I have been thinking," Ashley began as she sat down on my rolling desk chair.

"That's a fantastic thing to do," Papa Pete said. "You never know what will happen when you think."

"This is serious, Papa Pete," Ashley said.

Papa Pete pretended like he had a zipper across his mouth and zipped it shut. He motioned for Ashley to continue.

"So Frankie and I have been thinking that the King Kahuna Huna costume could use a little work."

"You're kidding?" I said, faking surprise.

"You don't like the LEGO boats hanging off my arms?"

"No, dude. I'm all for LEGO boats," Frankie said, "if you're four and in the bathtub. The thing is, Zip, we're trying to class up the act. Make it slick."

"We want the costumes to be more authentic," Ashley said. "King Kahuna Huna should be wearing palm leaves and coconuts and Hawaiian flowers."

"And where are we going to get that stuff?" I asked.

Papa Pete raised his hand, and we let him unzip his lips.

"Big Eddie's Costume Store," he said. "It just so happens Big Eddie is one of the Chopped Livers."

The Chopped Livers are Papa Pete's bowling team. I don't mean to brag, but they've been number one in the Senior Bowling League at McKelty's Roll 'N Bowl for three years straight.

"A costume store," Ashley said. "Great idea. Can you take us there?"

"Let me make a call," Papa Pete said.

He went into the living room and came back

two minutes later with a big smile on his face.

"Big Eddie officially closed the shop ten minutes ago, but he said he'd stay open for a while as a special favor."

"Big Eddie sounds like a real stand-up guy," Frankie said.

"Naturally," said Papa Pete. "He's a Chopped Liver."

When I told my parents where we were going, I was worried that they'd make us take Emily and Robert along. But luckily, the geek and geekess were busy in Emily's room, trying to teach Bruce the Gecko his dance moves for the talent show. They were having trouble because every time they had his little front legs hooked on the toothpick they were using to keep him upright so he could dance on his back legs, he fell off. Then he'd scoot under the lettuce leaf and hide. I guess geckos just weren't cut out for ballroom dancing.

We dashed out of the building before Emily and Robert changed their minds. Big Eddie's was a couple of blocks away, near the corner of Amsterdam and 71st. Papa Pete walks fast, and we had to skip to keep up with him. Correction.

Ashley skipped. Frankie and I jogged. We're not really the skipping type.

Big Eddie's is a tiny stop, sandwiched in between Royal Dry Cleaners and a Chinese take-out restaurant. When we got there, we stopped in front to look in the window. It was jam-packed with really cool stuff like vampire masks and fake blood capsules and slimy green monster hands and plastic fangs.

Suddenly, the door to the store flew open and a huge man who filled the entire doorway popped his head out. He was wearing a patch over one eye, and had a bloody scar running all the way down his cheek.

"Help!" he shouted. "I'm bleeding!"

Ashley screamed. Frankie and I jumped backward. Papa Pete burst out laughing.

"Papa Pete, he's hurt," I said.

"You mean this?" the giant man said, pointing to his bleeding scar. "I'll recover. Watch!"

He reached up to his cheek and with a big yank, pulled the bloody scar off. It was plastic!

"Kids, I'd like you to meet Big Eddie," Papa Pete said. "Fellow Chopped Liver and all-around prankster."

Big Eddie pulled the patch off his eye (the patch was fake, too) and held out his hand to shake. I squeezed it and a buzzer went off. What kind of grown-up wears a trick buzzer in his palm?

"Come on in, kids," he said. "I hear you're looking for Hawaiian costumes. Right this way."

He took us over to a section that had grass skirts and coconut bikini tops, plastic palm leaves and necklaces of pink Hawaiian flowers. Frankie and Ashley dove into the stuff like it was buried treasure. There wasn't enough room for me to look, too, so I wandered around the store. What a fun place! I tried on some snaggly teeth that made me look like Nick McKelty. Thank goodness I didn't smell like him, too. After that, I tried on a black, shiny cape and a Dracula wig.

"I vant to suck your blood," I said into the mirror, in my Count Dracula accent that I've been practicing since before I even knew what a vampire was.

On the top shelf, I noticed a big, crazy gray wig with hair flying out from all sides. I jumped as high as I could and grabbed it down. When I slid it on, you could barely see my face because of the gray hair shooting out in all directions.

"Check this out," I said to Papa Pete. "I look like Albert Einstein."

"If it's Einstein you want, come with me," Big Eddie said. He took me to another counter where he handed me a furry gray mustache and a collar with a fluffy old-fashioned bow tie attached to it. I put the collar around my T-shirt and stuck the mustache on my upper lip.

"I vill now tell you about zee universe," I said in a pretty terrible German accent. I think I sounded more like Count Dracula than like Albert Einstein, but I didn't care because I was having so much fun.

Then it hit me.

Wait a minute, Hank. WAIT A MINUTE! Oh yeah, this is a genius idea.

I looked over at Papa Pete. He had a special twinkle in his eye.

"Are you thinking what I'm thinking?" I asked him.

"Depends on what you're thinking," said Papa Pete.

"I'm thinking that I could do my Einstein report dressed up as him. *I vill discuss zee theory of relativity dressed as Einstein zee genius.*"

Big Eddie burst out laughing.

"You got a lot of imagination, kid," he said.

Yes, imagination. That was the key. Didn't Einstein himself say "imagination is more important than knowledge"?

Frankie and Ashley bought some plastic Hawaiian flowers and palm leaves. Me, I bought the collar and bow tie, the wig and the mustache. And a bottle of something called spirit gum, which Big Eddie said is what real actors use to stick fake hair on their skin. I didn't want my mustache falling off in the middle of my report.

If I had been the skipping type, I would have skipped out of Big Eddie's store. I felt fantastic. Suddenly, I couldn't wait until Friday. I was going to morph into Albert Einstein, right in front of my summer-school class. I would be *zee great man of zee science world.*

It would be just like Mr. Rock said—I was going to become the famous person I admired. I would get an A for sure. As Albert Einstein him-self would say, *it was in zee bag.*

CHAPTER 15

Of courſe, I ſtill had to study. I knew that. I wasn't going to get an A on my report just by standing up and talking in a bad German accent with a crazy wig on. But wouldn't it be great if things could really happen that way in real life?

So I spent the next two days at school hard at work on my project. On Wednesday, I brought my library books to class in a shopping bag, and Mr. Rock helped me read them during free time. I took notes on index cards, so I'd remember the important parts of Einstein's life and his theories when I got up to give my report.

The more I learned about Albert Einstein, the more I liked him. I'm not sure exactly how, but his theory of relativity showed that time travel to the future is actually possible if you fly fast enough through space. Where do I get a ticket? Also, he refused to wear socks because they would get holes in them. I am so glad he can't open my sock drawer. Anyway, those are both pretty interesting facts, if you ask me.

"Hank, I'm really proud of the way you're working," Mr. Rock said to me on Thursday, right before lunch.

That made Joelle mad. She had been especially crabby since Mr. Rock took away her cell phone.

"What about me?" she said. "My work is way better than his."

She was doing her report on a famous gymnast named Mary Lou Retton who won an Olympic Gold Medal. All Joelle was doing, though, was drawing pictures of her in different-colored leotards.

Before Mr. Rock could answer Joelle, a fifth-grader named Lauren let out a scream from the other side of the room.

"What's wrong, Lauren?" Mr. Rock asked.

"Luke Whitman is trying to smell my lunch!"

Mr. Rock left us in a hurry to try to get Luke's nose out of Lauren's lunch bag.

Joelle leaned over to me. "Your handwriting

looks like a monkey wrote it," she whispered.

"At least I'm writing important facts," I snapped. "You're just coloring tights."

"For your information, I'm going to be a world-famous leotard designer when I grow up," she said. "My boyfriend, Nick, says I'm going to make a million dollars."

"Right, and my name is Bernice."

"Why do you always say that?" she said. "Your name isn't Bernice."

I could see that Joelle and Nick had the same sense of humor, which, by the way, does not exist.

By the time lunch came around, I couldn't wait to get away from her. I went out on the playground to see if I could hang out with Frankie and Ashley, but the Junior Explorers had gone over to the pool at the Paris Hotel up the street for swimming lessons. So I went back to class, got my Einstein book, and sat down at one of the lunch tables to read.

That's right, you heard me correctly. I was reading. By choice. For fun. Well, maybe not for fun, but still, it's pretty amazing, huh?

"What are you reading, Hank?"

It was my little pal, Mason.

"Hey, Mason. This is a book on Albert Einstein."

"He has funny hair."

"I agree, dude, but under that hair, he's got quite a brain."

"Why?"

Mason pulled himself up on the bench and sat next to me. He didn't just sit next to me, he snuggled right in close to me and put his head on my shoulder so he could see the pictures in the book. By the way, if you're keeping track, that's the twelfth cutest thing about kindergartners. When they sit next to you, they snuggle like little puppies.

So I read to him. Wow, that was a first. I was actually reading to someone else. If I got stuck on a word, I'd take a guess, and that was good enough for Mason. Amazing as it seems, there were plenty of words I did know how to read, and he seemed to really like hearing them. We read about where Einstein was born and his two children. We read about how he became the most famous scientist in the world. We read how he liked to play the violin, and that he even gave his violin a name. He called it Lina. We read how he loved to do puzzles and sail on boats. And we learned that even though his theories led to the creation of the atomic bomb, Einstein himself said, "I am willing to fight for peace."

Mason didn't move a muscle the whole time I read to him. He just sat there listening. And me, I had only one thought:

Look at me, world. I'm reading to someone else. I just can't get over it!!!

CHAPTER 16

That night after dinner, Frankie, Ashley, and I met in the clubhouse for what Frankie called a dress rehearsal of our magic trick. Frankie loves to be prepared. He would have made a great Cub Scout except that he wouldn't like wearing that yellow scarf. If the Cub Scouts would ever decide to lose the scarf, Frankie's in.

"Okay, guys," he said, checking his watch. "In exactly twenty and one half hours we're going to wow 'em and zow 'em. Ashweena, talk to me."

"Costume, completed," said Ashley. She twirled around to show us her blue pants and top that she had covered with green rhinestones in the shape of ocean waves. There were yellow rhinestones for the sun, and red rhinestones for coconuts. She was very sparkly.

"Princess Leilani, you look great," Frankie said. "Music all set?"

"Ukulele, tuned," Ashley answered, strumming the first notes of her crazy *hooky lau* song. "All four strings pulled tight."

"Zip, where are you?" Frankie called out. "Report in."

I had been standing behind a column of cardboard boxes, where I had gone to change into my costume. I had the green velvet pillows strapped on my feet and the palm leaves we got at Big Eddie's wrapped around my waist. I had tried to tie the coconuts around my upper arms, but it was hard, using only one hand and my teeth. I stepped out from behind the boxes and raised my arms in a very kingly manner.

"Your coconuts are sagging," Ashley said.

"So help me. There's only so much a guy can do with his teeth."

I took a step over to Ashley, but I had forgotten about my pillow shoes. I tripped over the boxes big time, and landed headfirst in the couch.

"King Kahuna Huna, your butt is flapping in the breeze," Frankie said, cracking up.

"Go ahead and laugh. I need a hand here, friends of mine."

Ashley and Frankie were laughing too hard to help, so that left me bent over like a pretzel, wedged between the cushions and the back of the couch. There was a lot of dust in that couch, and when I breathed in, it flew all the way up to the top of my nose.

Ah . . . ah . . . ah . . . ah-choo!

Man, I sneezed so hard that the force of it unwedged my head. That made Frankie and Ashley laugh even harder. I have to admit, it was pretty funny. I laughed too.

"Can we be serious here?" I said, after I had caught my breath. "I want to finish in time to rehearse my Einstein speech. If I blow that, King Kahuna Huna is a no-show."

"Zip, you're freaking yourself out," Frankie said.

"I'm a little nervous," I confessed. "There's a lot of information to remember."

"You've got it all written down on note cards," Ashley said. "You'll be fine."

"You'd be fine, Ash, but I may not be."

"Zip, what's the rule?" Frankie asked,

looking me in the eyeballs.

"Breathe," I answered.

"Right. Take air in through your nose and let it out through your mouth. Remember, oxygen is power."

"I know."

"Don't just know. Do."

I took a deep yoga-style breath, the way Frankie's mom, who is a yoga teacher, had always taught us to do. I must have dislodged some of the dust that was still hanging around up there in my nose, because I sneezed so hard, my coconuts sagged again.

"Let's run through our act before you lose your coconuts altogether," Frankie said.

The rehearsal was a little shaky, but we got through it. Ashley strummed her ukulele and danced, and Frankie did a few magic chants that he made up himself. When he said the magic word, *zengawii*, I leaped out from behind the couch. Of course, at the actual talent show, I was going to leap out from a cloud of lava smoke. We were going to use chunks of dry ice and pour water on them to create the lava smoke. We couldn't rehearse that part in our clubhouse, because kids can't handle dry ice themselves. It can burn you if you touch it. I think it's so strange that ice can burn you from being too cold, but trust me, it's true. Ashley's mom and dad had agreed to bring the dry ice to the playground for us. They're both doctors, so it was really nice of them to come home early to help. I guess that's why Papa Pete calls them the good doctors Wong.

After we finished our Magik 3 rehearsal, Ashley and Frankie sat down on the couch to listen to me go through my Einstein report. It was getting near bedtime, so I didn't take the time to change into my Einstein costume. I have to confess, it felt a little strange to be talking like a German scientist while wearing nothing but palm leaves and foot pillows.

Maybe it was the Kahuna Huna costume that distracted me. My German accent wasn't bad, but I just couldn't keep my facts straight. Even though I had written them down on index cards, it was like my eyes were looking at the sentences, but my brain was jumbling them up. I kept tripping over my words like my tongue was too big for my mouth.

"I can't do this!" I yelled out, when I couldn't pronounce the word *relativity* three times in a row.

"Remember the Big B, dude," Frankie said.

"Frankie, what are you talking about?"

"Breathe, Zip. Breathe!"

I took a breath.

"The word is *re-la-tiv-i-ty*," Ashley said, pronouncing it really slowly. "Come on. You know it, Hank."

I settled down and kept going. Finally, I came to the end of the report.

"What did you think, guys?" I said, flopping down on the couch, exhausted. "Will I get an A?"

Ashley didn't answer. My heart started to beat faster.

Frankie jumped in. "It's definitely a B-plus. And that is a great grade, dude."

B-plus? No, not a B-plus.

Without another word, I jumped up from the couch, ran out of the clubhouse to the elevator, and started pushing the button about a hundred times, hoping that would make the elevator come faster.

I rode upstairs rehearsing—not my Einstein speech but what I was going to say to my father. I had to convince him that a B-plus was good enough to let me go to the luau. He had to say yes.

Hey, I'm not proud. If I had to beg, I would.

CHAPTER 17

TEN WAYS TO BEG YOUR DAD TO SAY YES WHEN HE WANTS TO SAY NO

1. Fall on the floor and pound the carpet, kicking and screaming. Whining is good too.

2. When he says, "Stop that right away," stand up, apologize, and say you were just kidding.

3. Make sure you end every sentence with, "Pretty please with a cherry on top."

4. Tell him it will be your pleasure to polish every pair of shoes he owns or ever will own, even tennis shoes and flip-flops. And no, there is no tipping required.

5. Promise him this is the last thing you'll ever ask for except maybe a car when you're sixteen and a new PlayStation

on your birthday. Oh yeah, and the video games that go with it, but only four of them. Okay, five. But after that, nothing.

6. Swear to keep his mechanical pencils always filled with fresh lead. (WARNING: If your dad isn't a crossword-puzzle freak like mine, this one may not work so well.)

7. Try a compliment. Tell him that he's not going bald, he just looks really good in very short hair.

8. Trust me, guilt works. Just mention that you know he loves your sister more than you, but it's okay, because you're fine with it. It only hurts a tiny little bit.

9. Don't try to scare him, but you might mention that if you don't get what you want, you may have to go lie down under your bed until you're forty-five.

10. Whimper like a puppy dog.

11. Go simple and just say please.***

***I can't believe that after all the time we've spent together, you're still surprised that there are eleven reasons on my list of ten. It's me, Hank. You know I can't count!

CHAPTER 18

Poor Hank

"**Dad, let's say** I only get a B-plus on my Einstein report. Could I still go to the luau and the sleepover?"

I was standing in our living room. He was sitting in his chair, doing a crossword puzzle. He didn't answer.

So I went into begging mode and ran through my list, each and every item. I begged so hard that a rock would have felt sorry for me.

When the first eleven reasons didn't work, I even added a twelfth. I told him it would make Cheerio so happy to see me at the luau. I figured maybe my dad could say no to me but not to our family dog, for heaven's sake.

And you know what?

Nothing worked.

You heard me. Nothing. Nada.

All Stan the Man said was, "The requirement was an A, Hank. You can do it if you try."

Thanks, Dad. No pressure there.

CHAPTER 19

The next morning, Frankie was full of energy as his dad walked us to school. Too full of energy, if you ask me. He was making me more nervous than I already was.

"So what time is your report?" he asked with a mouthful of chocolate donut.

"I don't know, sometime after lunch."

"You can't be late, Zip. We go on first in the talent show."

"My dad promised he'd be there when school lets out. If Mr. Rock gives him good news, I'll be at the talent show."

"And if not?" Frankie stuffed the rest of his donut into his mouth all at once. "Maybe we should have had a backup plan."

"Thanks for the confidence," I said.

"You're right. It's all about confidence. You'll be there. Won't he, Ashweena?"

Ashley wasn't listening. She was busy hopping over puddles made by the street-cleaning truck to make sure she didn't get her costume dirty. Frankie and I were carrying our costumes in grocery bags. His mom was going to bring everyone's sleeping bags later. Ashley was wearing her costume. She had worked hard on it, and she wanted to show off her colorful rhinestone work.

We headed down one block east on 78th Street where our school is. The Junior Explorers were already gathering in front. Most of the kids were dressed in their luau costumes. Nick McKelty was wearing these horrible purple and orange flowered swimming trunks and flip-flops as big as the Brooklyn Bridge. I don't mean to gross you out, but his toenails were as long and as snaggly as his front teeth.

Miss Cell Phone Joelle was there, too, wearing a bright pink leotard with weird, brightly colored shapes painted all over it. I'm no leotard expert, but if those are the kind she designs, I'm not seeing a million dollars in her future.

I could see her checking out Ashley's costume as we walked up. "Eeuuww, rhinestones," she said to Ashley. "That is so a year-and-a-half ago!"

I wanted to tell her what I thought of her stupid outfit, but my friend Ashley Wong has quite a mouth on her, and she can take care of herself.

"I'm so sorry about your leotard," Ashley said to her. "It looks like you must have spilled paint on it."

"I made this design myself," Joelle said. "For your information, these are birds of paradise, a native Hawaiian bird."

"For your information, the birds of paradise in Hawaii are flowers, not actual birdies, Miss Bird Brain," Ashley said.

That's my Ashweena. She shoots, she scores!

Emily and Robert were waiting on the front steps with the other Junior Explorers. Emily had insisted that my mom walk them to school early so Bruce the Gecko could get used to the environment. She didn't want him to stress out—she was concerned about his mental state. If you ask me, she should be concerned about her own mental state, which I would describe as totally weird and scaly.

Robert was leaning over Bruce's plastic box, talking to him. I wonder what you would say to a gecko, anyway?

"Hey, geck, how was that cricket you had for breakfast? Juicy enough for you?"

Robert was wearing swimming trunks and a white tank top. It occurred to me that I had never seen his arms before. They looked like toothpaste that had squirted out of the tube, all squiggly. Bruce the Gecko was probably staring up at Robert, shaking like the leaf of lettuce he was standing on. Could you blame him? If you saw Robert Upchurch in swimming trunks and a tank top that was two sizes too big, you'd shake like a leaf of lettuce, too.

"Hank! Mommy, it's Hank!"

I turned around to see Mason running down the street at full speed. He was waving his arms and shouting my name. When he reached me, he threw himself full force into my kneecaps.

"Hey, Mason. What's up?" I said.

"I have peanut butter for lunch."

"Good for you. Peanut butter rocks, dude."

Mason's mom came running up after him.

I assumed it was his mom because she had red curly hair just like his.

"You must be Hank," she said, putting out her hand to shake mine. "Mason talks about you all the time."

"He's a cool kid," I said.

"What's in your grocery bag?" Mason asked me. "Can I see?"

"It's my Einstein costume," I said. "Today is my report."

"Can I come?"

"I'll ask your teacher if it's okay," Mason's mom told him. "That is, if it's all right with you, Hank."

"Sure. I just hope I don't mess it up."

"Oh, I'm sure you won't," Mason's mom said. "Last night at dinner Mason told us all about Albert Einstein and said you taught him everything. You must be a very intelligent young man."

Nick McKelty was standing nearby, and that was all he needed to hear.

"That's a hoot!" he said. "Zipper Zitt is a first-class moron. He's so stupid, he had to go to summer school."

Mason's mother wheeled around and stared McKelty right in the eye.

"Perhaps one day you'll learn to be as kind as Hank is," she said.

I looked at McKelty to see what he was going to do. It's one thing to talk back to a kid. It's another thing to open up a mouth to an adult. I could see his big, slow brain grinding away, trying to make a decision and finally grinding to a halt.

Ms. Adolf appeared on the steps, clapping her hands three times. She was wearing her gray shirt with the coconut bikini top over it. This time, it didn't even surprise me to see her dressed like that. It's amazing what the human brain can get used to.

"Aloha and welcome to our luau extravaganza and sleepover, pupils," she said. "I am disappointed to have to tell you that Principal Love can't be with us today. He threw his back out while doing the limbo."

Everyone just stared at her, trying to picture short Principal Love bent over backward, inching his way under a broomstick.

"However, I am happy to report that I will

be filling his shoes and leading the festivities this afternoon."

Everyone groaned.

"And what was that? A group groan? Now all Junior Explorers will follow me to the Hawaiian Islands," she said. "Summer-schoolers, to your classrooms."

Mason's mom took his hand and started into the building, but then she stopped and turned to me.

"What time is your report, Hank?" she asked.

"After lunch."

"I'll try to arrange for Mason to come," she said.

"Goody!" Mason shouted, starting to jump up and down like a monkey on a trampoline. "Goody gumdrops! Blue ones!"

I think you know what I'm going to say. The thirteenth cutest thing about kindergartners is that they say stuff like "goody gumdrops" and "silly willy" and "noodle nose," and they don't worry that anyone's going to make fun of them.

As I started in for class, I felt Frankie's hand on my shoulder.

"Listen, you're going to be great," he said. "Just focus, Zip. Be Albert Einstein. Keep your head in the game, Hank."

"We're counting on you," Ashley said.

"King Kahuna Huna will do as he is told," I said. "Count on it."

I sounded really confident. I just wished I felt that way, too.

CHAPTER 20

I spent the whole morning reviewing my notes in class. I read those index cards over and over until I knew every word. I was ready.

A few kids did their reports before lunch. Lauren, the fifth-grader, picked a famous opera singer named Marian Anderson and actually sang her whole report. Joelle made fun of her and called her a squeak box, but I thought she had a really pretty voice and was very brave to sing her report. Mr. Rock shouted bravo and said it was a spectacular performance. Of course, he is the music teacher.

Luke Whitman went next. He did his report on his uncle Wayne, who is a professional juggler in a traveling circus in Indiana. Luke told us that his uncle specializes in juggling lawn mowers and light farm equipment. Unfortunately, when Luke tried to do a juggling demonstration using cantaloupes, he dropped them and they cracked open and splattered all across the floor. Mr. Rock didn't even get mad. He said it was a quick way to make fruit salad. While Luke was cleaning up the mess, good old Joelle put up her hand and asked Luke if Uncle Wayne ever needed any new leotards to wear in his act. Luke told her he was a lawn mower juggler not a ballet dancer, and Joelle stuck her tongue out at him. I won't even tell you what he did back to her, but it involved his finger and his nose.

After lunch I asked Mr. Rock if it was okay if I missed Salvatore's report so I could go to the bathroom and prepare for mine. I knew that Salvatore was talking about Derek Jeter, who plays for the Yankees, and his report would just get me riled up anyway because I'm such a huge Mets fan.

I went into the bathroom with my grocery bag and lined my stuff up along the sink counter. I changed into a black T-shirt and put the collar with the floppy bow tie over it. Then I put on a suit jacket that I had worn to my cousin's wedding last year. I was wearing shorts on the bottom, which did look a little strange.

Too bad I hadn't thought to bring long pants. But when I looked in the mirror, I thought, *Yeah, Hank, you look like a German scientist . . . from the neck down and waist up, anyway.*

Next it was time for the wig and the mustache. I carefully took the bottle of spirit gum out of its plastic package. Big Eddie had told me to paint a little of it on my upper lip and then wait a minute for it to get sticky before putting on the mustache. While I was waiting for it to dry, I put on the wig. Wow, it was a lot of hair. You couldn't even see my face. I looked like a copy of a Neanderthal man I saw once in a diorama at the Museum of Natural History. I pulled the wig back on my head and yanked it right off. There I was, staring at me again in the mirror.

I decided to put a little of the spirit gum at my temples and over my ears. Not too much. Just enough to hold the wig on.

Good thinking, Hank. Maybe you should be a makeup artist in the movies when you grow up. Wig-gluer to the stars. I like the sound of that.

I touched my upper lip, and it was pretty

sticky. Man, that spirit gum was strong. I took the mustache out of its little plastic case and stuck it above my lip. It looked like a huge, furry caterpillar had gotten loose and was crawling under my nose. It tickled too, but I didn't dare rub it, or it would get all crooked on me.

I looked at myself in the mirror.

Maybe this is what I'm going to look like when I'm Papa Pete's age.

"Hello, Hankie," I said to myself in the mirror. "I am zee grandfazzer of zee science vorld."

I started laughing, but it was hard because my upper lip was stiff from the spirit gum.

Come on, Hank. Stay focused. Remember what Frankie said. Keep your head in the game. Magik 3 is counting on you.

I wiped the grin off my face and picked up the wig. Bending over, I shoved my head into it and held the sides down where I had put the spirit gum on my temples. I looked up and there he was, Albert himself. Hair flying, mustache glued, bow tie covering my Adam's apple.

I smiled a little. This was going to be great.

All I had to do was clean up, get back to class, and get my A.

I picked up the bottle of spirit gum and was just about to twist the cap back on when the door flew open.

"Hank! It's me!"

Mason came charging full speed at me like a galloping pony, flinging himself into my knee-caps. Oooooph! The bottle of spirit gum went flying into the air and as I reached to catch it, it turned upside down. Spirit gum oozed out all over my hands.

"Oh, no!" I screamed.

"I'm sorry, Hank," Mason said.

Before I could answer him, the door flew open again. It was Luke Whitman.

"Come on, Hank. Salvatore is done, and we're all waiting for you. Mr. Rock wants you to come right this second."

Studied Violin
Munich, Germany
Bored at school
Born in 1879

CHAPTER 21

I ran toward the classroom, giving my hands a quick wipe on the back of my shorts. Mason followed behind. All the kids were waiting for me as I bolted into class. Before I could even try to explain what had happened with the spirit gum, Mr. Rock took one look at me and burst into applause. For a second, I wondered why he was clapping. Then I remembered that I was wearing my costume.

"Ladies and gentleman, let's give a warm welcome to Albert Einstein, twentieth-century genius and man of science," he said.

"And man of ugly hair," Joelle called out. "You'd think he would've invented the brush."

Everyone laughed.

"I don't like her," Mason whispered to me.

"That makes two of us," I whispered back.

Mr. Rock pulled up a chair for Mason and

took a seat next to him.

"Go ahead, Albert," he said. "Tell us all about yourself."

I took my place in front of the class and pulled out the note cards from my pocket.

Calm down, Hank, and focus. Breathe. You are Albert. Be Albert.

The information was right there in front of me. All I had to do was erase the spirit gum spill from my mind. I took a deep breath and began.

"I vas born in Germany in zee year of 1879. Mine mothzzer vas Pauline, and mine farzzer vas Hermann."

I looked around the room. The kids seemed to be enjoying my accent. Everyone was smiling—everyone but Joelle, that is. She was picking some lint off one of the birdies on her leotard.

I had finished the facts that were on the first note card, and it was time to go to the next. I reached down to shuffle the top card to the back of the pile. It stuck to my fingers. I shook my hand, hoping it would fall off, but it didn't. The spirit gum was starting to dry and get sticky, just like Big Eddie said it would.

The card just needs a little help getting off my finger, that's all.

I bent over and put the card on the floor. Then I stepped on it with my sneaker and yanked my hand away. The card came free from my hand but stuck to my sneaker. I left it there. I was no fool. I wasn't going to touch it again.

Where was I? Oh, yeah. Albert goes to school.

"I vas raised in Munich, where I vent to school and studied zee violin. I didn't enjoy zee school much. I found it—how you kids say—too boring."

"I'm with you, Big Al," Luke Whitman called out.

Good, Hank. They're liking it. Move to the next card.

This time, I carefully picked up card number two using only the tippy tips of my first two fingers. I thought I could just slide it to the back of the pile. Unfortunately, the card didn't cooperate. It stuck to the tippy tip of my index finger, which by now was really sticky. The spirit gum was kicking in big time.

Don't panic, Hank. Just remove the card from your finger and go on.

I took my other hand and carefully pulled the card off my index finger. It came off—only now it was stuck to my other hand. I could hear Salvatore and Matthew laughing in the back of the class.

"Zis is part of my plan," I said. "Not to worry."

I raised my hand to my mouth, put the index card between my teeth, clamped down, and pulled on it like a dog grabbing for a bone. It came flying off my finger, all right. But now it was stuck to my tooth.

Did you ever try to give a report with an index card hanging off your chompers? Trust me, it makes things very complicated.

A few more kids started to laugh. I had to get that thing out of my mouth quickly. So I reached up with my whole hand and grabbed the card impatiently. No more Mister Nice Guy. I think my hands might have been shaking from being nervous, because I missed the card and grabbed my mustache instead. Three of my fingers instantly attached themselves to the fake hair on my upper lip.

I had a choice. I could either try to continue my speech with three fingers clinging to my upper lip, or I could try to detach my hand from my mustache. It was a no-brainer. I pulled.

Uh-oh. What's that?

I reached up to my face and realized that I had yanked the mustache too hard. Half of it had slid down my lip and landed on my teeth. I have to tell you, it felt pretty hairy in my mouth. And it was really crowded in there, too. I had three fingers, an index card, and half a mustache all fighting for space. Plus two new molars. It's amazing I still had room for my tongue!

Everyone was laughing now. Mason was giggling so hard, he nearly fell off his chair. If I hadn't needed an A, it would have been funny to me, too. But under the circumstances, I couldn't laugh. I had no choice but to continue.

With my fingers and mustache filling my mouth, and the card I needed still in my teeth, I had to do the rest of the report from memory. The problem was, my memory wasn't working.

"I am very famous for developing zee theory

of vhat you call it," I said. See what I mean? I told you my memory was on vacation.

"You know, zee big deal theory about zee light and all zat stuff." Man, I was desperate.

You're losing it, Hankster. There it goes.

Suddenly, a little voice chirped up like a bird.

"You mean the theory of relativity."

It was Mason! He remembered!

Way to go, little dude.

"Zat is exactly vhat I mean," I said. "Zank you, young man."

I thought it would be good to act casual at this point in my presentation, so I strolled over to the desk and leaned against the edge of it like Mr. Rock often does.

"My greatest discovery vas vhen I calculated zee speed limit of zee universe, known as zee speed of light, vhich is . . ."

Oh, no. I was drawing another blank. Come on, brain. Give me a little help here!

The speed of light had left my brain at the speed of light. For the life of me, I couldn't remember the numbers. I could almost see them written down on my note card in green ink. I just couldn't get them to jump off the card and into my head.

The note cards! I could still look at them. I glanced down at the stack of index cards that were clutched tightly in my hands. I should say clutched in my sticky hands, *sticky* being the key word here. The index cards were all clumped up in one big wad, sealed together forever with spirit gum. Somewhere in that wad was the speed of light, but it was buried deep.

The class was staring at me, waiting for me to say something. I thought that maybe if I started fresh, the information would just pop into my head. It does that sometimes.

"So like I vas saying, I figured out zee speed of light, vhich is . . ."

Nope, nothing popped into my head. No popping, just silence. Suddenly, I heard that little chirping voice speak up again. It was Mason!

"The speed of light is one hundred and eighty-six thousand miles per second," he said, like it was something that every kindergartner knew.

Mason Harris Jerome Dunn. You are amazing, dude!

"Zank you again, young man," I said. "I vas just seeing if everyone vas avake. And you are. Also, you're a very intelligent person."

"No, I'm not." Mason giggled. "You taught me that, Hank. I mean Albert."

From the corner of my eye, I saw Mr. Rock hold out his hand and give Mason a high five.

"Go on, Einstein," Mr. Rock said. "We're very interested."

"Nothing goes faster than zee speed of light," I continued. "If you could go faster zan zat, vhich is impossible, you vould get sick in zee tummy unt get a speeding ticket, too."

I had planned that joke. And it was working. Everyone chuckled, and for a second I felt good again. But only for a second. I had forgotten one little detail—the spirit gum all over the back of my shorts.

When I stepped away from the desk to make my next point, I heard a loud ripping sound. It sounded like my pants ripping all the way across the butt area.

That's because it WAS my pants ripping all the way across the butt area. "I don't believe this!" Joelle howled. "Wait until I tell Nick!"

I looked over at the desk and saw a good portion of my shorts clinging to the edge. That meant only one thing—that a good portion of my tighty whities were hanging out for all the class to see.

What would Albert Einstein do?

Run, that's what. Which is exactly what I did. Sideways, all the way to the door.

CHAPTER 22

"Hank, come out."

I was huddled in the stall of the boys' bathroom. Mr. Rock was on the other side of the door, talking to me as I wrapped myself up in the palm leaves from my King Kahuna Huna costume. Thank goodness for that grocery bag with my costume in it. Without it, my tighty whities would still have been waving in the breeze.

"Thanks, anyway, Mr. Rock, but I think I'll just hang out in here for a while, if you don't mind."

"I do mind," he said.

"What happened out there was pretty embarrassing," I explained. "I'd rather not have to see all the kids right now."

"I don't expect you to go back in to class," he said. "Just come out of the stall."

"No, thanks. I like small spaces. It's cozy in here."

"Hank."

"No, really. All it needs is a fireplace."

"Hank, why won't you come out?"

"Because if I do, I'll have to see Frankie and Ashley and I can't face them, either. I've messed everything up for them, too."

"I just saw Frankie," Mr. Rock said. "He stopped by the classroom to say he was expecting you at the luau."

"I know he's counting on me, but I can't go," I told Mr. Rock. "My dad said the only way I could go was if I got an A on my Einstein report."

"Oh," Mr. Rock answered. "Well, I'm afraid you didn't get an A."

"Tell me something I don't know."

"You got an A-plus."

My ears almost stood up on my head and danced the cha-cha. I opened the door and stuck my head out of the stall.

"You didn't happen to say that I got an A-plus, did you, Mr. Rock?"

He smiled. "That's exactly what I said,

Hank. I gave you an A for knowing the material and for creativity of presentation. And the plus was for being able to teach what you know to someone else."

"You mean Mason?"

"Yes." Mr. Rock nodded. "After you left the room, Mason finished your report for you. He told us about how Einstein won the Nobel Prize and loved to sail boats and how the Hopi Indians gave him the name 'The Great Relative.'"

"And did he tell you that Einstein didn't wear socks because his big toenail always made a hole in them?"

"Yes, he did," smiled Mr. Rock. "I could hear your voice in every word he said, Hank. You're a fine teacher and a natural communicator."

Let me just take a minute to describe to you how I felt when Mr. Rock said that. Imagine that some people gave you the biggest, best birthday present you ever hoped for in your whole entire life. And then they rolled out a birthday cake the size of a jet airplane. A chocolate cake with chocolate frosting and chocolate sprinkles. And then they gave you a spoon and said you could eat the whole cake yourself. And when you were done, you could play with your new present for the rest of the year. That would feel pretty cool, huh?

Well, that's how I felt. Imagine it. A teacher, *my* teacher, gave me a real live compliment for schoolwork I had done. And an A-plus for something I never thought I could do in the first place! Unbelievable.

"Wow," I said to Mr. Rock. "Wowee, wow, wow, wow."

How's that for being a natural communicator?

"I've already discussed your grade with your father," Mr. Rock said. "So if I'm not mistaken, I think you have a luau and a sleepover to go to."

"What time is it?" I asked.

"Two-thirty," he answered.

Two-thirty! The talent show started at two-thirty! And Magik 3 was on first.

I shot out of the bathroom stall like a torpedo.

"Hank!" Mr. Rock called after me. "Your wig!"

I had forgotten that I was still Albert Einstein

from the waist up. I gave the wig a tug as I bolted for the playground. Oh boy, that spirit gum had really worked. The Einstein hair was on there for good, maybe even longer. No time to get it off now. That went for the droopy mustache, as well.

Albert Einstein, meet King Kahuna Huna. I hope you two dudes get along, because you're going to be spending some quality time together.

CHAPTER 23

I was panting pretty hard by the time I reached the far end of the playground where the luau was taking place. All the Junior Explorers were sitting on striped beach blankets in front of a stage that had been put up for the talent show. The backdrop of the stage was painted in a Hawaiian scene with purple volcanoes and red lava. Next to that, there was a limbo area set up in the sandbox. And next to that was a big wading pool filled with water and floating plastic Hawaiian flowers. I've never been to Hawaii, but I have to say, if it looks anything like the playground at PS 87 looked, I would really enjoy it.

There was no time for stopping to admire the scenery, though. Frankie was already on stage wearing a top hat and a Hawaiian shirt. He was talking into a microphone that crackled a little when he spoke.

"Come with me now to the ancient Hawaiian Islands, when King Kahuna Huna sailed the seas in his magical canoe," I heard him say.

Yikes. That was me. I had better get sailing, or I was going to be up a creek without a paddle.

Ashley was standing on the stage strumming her ukulele and singing softly.

"*Oh, we're going to a hooky lau, a hooky, hooky, hooky, hooky, hooky lau.*"

I know it was a crazy song, but with the volcano and the lava and the Hawaiian flowers, it all kind of worked.

Her dad, Dr. Wong, was using tongs to put big chunks of dry ice into a bucket on the stage in front of where the volcano was painted. Ashley's mom, the other Dr. Wong, was standing by with a kettle of water. They were concentrating very hard on what they were doing, so that when I talked to them, they didn't even look up.

"Dr. Wong?" I said.

"Yes, Hank," they both answered at once.

I wondered if it was a problem to have the same name. Maybe Ashley's mom should go by Dr. Wongette so they wouldn't get confused. Or maybe Dr. Wongess sounds better. Or maybe something different like Dr. Mom-Wong.

Stop it, brain. No wondering now. We're in a hurry. Focus.

"Where should I go for my entrance?" I asked them.

"Backstage," the good doctors Wong answered together. "You're late."

Dr. Wongette poured some water from the kettle onto the dry ice in the bucket. She did a really good job because big puffs of white steam started to rise from it. I looked up at Frankie on stage. He was waving his magic wand and starting to do a tribal warrior dance.

"Oh Great King Kahuna Huna," he chanted as he danced, "come to us in your canoe. Appear in great clouds of smoke erupting from the Mauna Kapapa volcano."

I dashed backstage. It sounded like I was going to have to erupt any second.

Backstage was nothing more than the playground behind the volcano backdrop. Thank goodness for Ashley. She had remembered to put my pillow shoes right where I could find them. I could hear Frankie building up to my entrance as I slipped my feet under the ribbon we had tied to each pillow.

"And now, ladies and gentlemen, the moment has come," he said, making his voice echo into the microphone. "We have called King Kahuna Huna here to dazzle you with his ability to travel through time. King Kahuna Huna, show yourself!"

Ashley started to strum furiously on her ukulele. Frankie held the microphone close to his mouth and made the sound of a drumroll. He is really good at imitating sounds. Even though I couldn't see the kids in the audience, I could tell from their gasps that the good doctors Wong had really kicked up the steam. I could hear the water splashing in the dry-ice bucket, and I could even see some of the steam creeping under the scenery toward me.

I took a deep breath and leaped forward, crashing through the purple volcano painted on the brown paper that Ashley and Frankie had borrowed from my mom's deli. As I burst onto the stage, I put on my biggest smile and held my arms up to the sky.

I have to say so myself, it was quite an

entrance. At first, all the kids were too stunned to say anything. It was totally silent in the audience.

Then everyone broke out laughing. I mean, they erupted!

"Zip," Frankie whispered to me, "what's with the hair and mustache?"

"I can explain that."

"No time now," Ashley whispered.

Frankie looked at the audience. They were still cracking up, which wasn't exactly what we had intended.

"You better come up with something, dude." Frankie said. "Make it good."

Okay, Hank. You've got a good imagination. Crank it up . . . immediately.

"Hello, mine little friends of PS 87," I said in my German accent. "Albert Einstein here."

"Hey, Zipper Butt, you're supposed to be King Kahuna Huna, jerk," Nick McKelty hollered out. He looked over at Joelle and gave her a punch in the arm. She shoved him back. Wow, they were perfect for each other. Mr. Hit and Ms. Shove.

"Zank you for bringing that up, chubby

head," I said, looking right at Nick. "I have a vonderful explanation."

"This is going to be lame," McKelty said.

"Vhile I vas riding around on a beam of light across zee universe, who should I bump into but King Kahuna Huna. He vas in his outer-space outrigger. And in case zat is too big a vord for you, McKelty, das is a canoe."

Everyone cracked up. McKelty turned red in the face, and I was loving it.

"Anyhoo," I went on, "zee king he says to me, 'Al . . . I need a big favor. I vas on my vay to PS 87 vhen I got a call that another volcano vas erupting on Waca Waca Wiki Waca.' For those of you who aren't a genius like me, zat's an island right next to Waca Wiki Wiki Waca."

I noticed that Kim Paulson and Katie Sperling, the two prettiest girls in my class, were holding their sides from laughing so hard. I didn't know people actually did that.

"So King Kahuna Huna says to me, 'I vas vondering if you could take over the PS 87 gig for me.' I said, 'Sure, Kahuna, das is my plea-sure.' So here I am."

The kids went wild. They burst into applause

and started to chant my name.

"Hank! Hank! Hank!" they shouted in a steady rhythm.

And here is the most incredible part: When I looked over at Ms. Adolf, she was laughing so hard, her coconuts had shifted all the way to her back.

Papa Pete always tells me, "Hankie, quit while you're ahead." So I did.

CHAPTER 24

They went on chanting my name for at least three minutes, maybe more. I could hear them as I shuffled backstage and took off my green pillow shoes.

"Good work, Zip," Frankie said. "You really pulled that from out of your hat."

"You mean his wig!" Ashley said, laughing.

Frankie, Ashley, and I came out and sat down in the front row of the audience. It was fun sitting there because a bunch of kids whispered to me that I was really funny.

It took a while for the audience to settle down so they could enjoy the next act, which was supposed to be Emily, Robert, and Bruce the Gecko. I don't know if it was the chanting from the kids or if you just can't teach a lizard to dance, but whatever the reason, Bruce had a freak-out. He curled himself up into a little ball that was so small it looked like a dot on top of the letter *i*. He hid in back of the cap from Robert's ear cream that was still being used as his water dish.

While everyone waited, Robert kneeled down next to Bruce's plastic box, begging him on his bony little knees.

"Come on, Bruce," he said. "I'll never ask anything of you again."

Bruce wasn't going for it. He stayed put. Robert tried another tactic.

"Actually, Bruce," he said, "I think you'll find that dancing is a very aerobic activity. It stimulates your heart and benefits your blood flow. You won't be sorry."

"Robert, don't pressure him," Emily said to him. "He's just a delicate little gecko."

I'm not someone who says nice things about my sister just for fun. But the truth is, I had to hand it to Emily. I mean, I felt badly for her that Bruce was a no-show. But it was pretty cool that she was willing to give up the talent contest for the good of the gecko. You've got to admire that kind of devotion to lizards.

McKelty was getting tired of waiting. He

stood up and shouted, "We've waited long enough. Let's lose the geeks. Who's ready to see the real winner?"

"Mr. McKelty," Ms. Adolf said, "there is another way to say you're ready."

"Gotcha, Ms. A." He smirked. "How about Make Way for the King?"

I felt someone pulling on my sleeve. I turned around, expecting to hear another compliment.

"Hi, Hank. You made me laugh."

It was none other than Micro-Mason, the cutest kid on the planet. Without saying another word, he crawled up on my lap and got comfortable so he could watch the rest of the show.

McKelty began to set up the stage for his act. I don't know what he was planning to do, but I could tell Joelle was part of it, too. He sent her to stand over by the wading pool with her dopey leotard on.

McKelty started to pull off his shirt. When he lifted his arms to get his shirt off, you could smell his stinky stink all the way over in the front row where we were sitting.

"He smells like my goldfish bowl," Mason said.

One thing about Mason, he sure doesn't sugarcoat the truth.

McKelty held up his hands to get everyone quiet, which we were anyway.

"Put your arms down," Mason said, holding his nose. I tried to cover his mouth with my hands, but it was too late. McKelty had heard him.

"Are you telling me what to do, shrimp?" McKelty said. Now I ask you, how much of a jerk do you have to be to say that to a little kid?

"Get on with it, McKelty," I said. "Show us your so-called talent."

"Here goes," said McKelty. "For my act, I am going to demonstrate the manly art of Frisbee Throwing on the Beach."

"Manly art, my foot," Ashley whispered. "Give me a break."

"I will demonstrate several techniques from my award-winning style," McKelty said.

"If this guy's ever won an award for anything, my name is Bernice," Frankie said.

"No, it's not," Mason said. "Hank says your name is Frankie."

McKelty took a red Frisbee out of a bowling

bag he had brought to the stage with him. He took a bunch of deep breaths and tried pumping up his arms like a bodybuilder.

"For my first trick, I will do the McKelty Special Long Toss," he said, spraying spit all the way to the first row. "Notice that not only will the Frisbee travel across the yard, it will change height three times as it travels."

That sounded pretty impressive. Everyone got really quiet as he prepared for the long toss.

"Joelle, are you ready to assist me?" McKelty called out.

"You bet I am," she giggled.

McKelty picked up the Frisbee with his huge, galumphy hand. He hauled back and flung it toward Joelle with all his might. I'll say this for McKelty. He's big, and when he throws a Frisbee, it sails.

Unfortunately for Joelle, it sailed right into her forehead, bonking her backward into the wading pool. She never even got her hands up to make the catch. Nope, she just plopped into the pool with a splash and a scream.

When she came up for air, she had a whole bunch of plastic Hawaiian flowers on her head.

Oh yeah, and about her leotard with the hand-painted birds of paradise all over—to put it simply, they were washed away.

Good work, McKelty. Now that's what I call a great trick.

Joelle didn't take it well. She started to pound the water with her palms, splashing everybody sitting anywhere near her.

"This is all your fault," she sputtered at Nick the Tick.

"My fault!" he yelled back at her. "How about catching it next time?"

Joelle hauled herself out of the pool and stormed off toward the auditorium. As she ran by us, you could hear her feet sloshing around in her sneakers.

"Hey, Joelle," Ashley said as she ran by, "you might try rhinestones next time. At least they're waterproof."

That pretty much put an end to McKelty's Frisbee act. After him, a few more kids performed. Heather Payne played "My Bonnie Lies Over the Ocean" on the cello. Kim Paulson and Katie Sperling did a lip sync to a Beatles song. Ben Brady cracked his knuckles in time to

"Battle Hymn of the Republic." He didn't just use his fingers. He used his toes, too. That takes talent. I was worried about him. He was going to give us some stiff competition.

After everyone was finished, Ms. Adolf had us all come to the stage and line up. She held her hand over each contestant's head and asked the audience to applaud for the one they thought was best. We went last, because we were the first to go on.

And guess what? We won!

As I looked out at all the kids applauding for us, and at Mason jumping up and down and screaming, I thought to myself, *Hank, this is the greatest day of your life.*

And here's the weird part: It happened in summer school.